HER
Billionaire
Inventor

dobi daniels

Luxhaven
Publishing

DEDICATION

To JC, Grandma D, and DC, whom I love more than life itself.

READ MORE BY DOBI DANIELS

Dexington Medical Billionaire Romance Series

Her Billionaire Inventor

Her Billionaire Internist

Her Billionaire Surgeon

Standalone

Her Billionaire Nemesis

SEE ALL OF DOBI DANIELS BOOKS
at smarturl.it/DobiDaniels

AUTHOR'S NOTE

Thank you for choosing HER BILLIONAIRE IN-VENTOR. Sarah Nash and Phillip Dexington are two characters that I absolutely love. They made their first appearance as parents when I wrote the first draft of HER BILLIONAIRE INTERNIST. I wondered about their own love story, and that's how HER BILLIONAIRE INVENTOR was born.

Having to deal with emotional scars is very common in the world we live in, and it is so easy to lose faith especially if those scars were inflicted by those dear to us. But learning how to trust again is typically difficult. I pray HER BILLIONAIRE INVENTOR gives you the hope to believe that love and trust is still possible, and gain the courage to take a chance on them again.

Please continue this journey with me in HER BIL-LIONAIRE INTERNIST, which is the follow-on story of Phillip and Sarah's child, Blake. To start reading, please visit smarturl.it/DobiDaniels.

Would you also want to be notified when the next book releases? Sign up at dobidaniels.com.

Once again, thank you so much for purchasing HER BILLIONAIRE INVENTOR and for meeting Sarah Nash and Phillip Dexington. If you enjoyed it, please consider leaving a review at smarturl.it/DobiDaniels or recommending it to a friend.

Thank you again for your support!

Dobi Daniels

HER

Billionaire

Inventor

CHAPTER ONE

Phillip Dexington placed his head in his hands. This was the nightmare he had been scared of, the one thing he had hoped to avoid with this product launch. He couldn't forget what had happened the last time. There had to be another way.

"Phillip, are you still there?" Bori's voice came loud and clear through the speakerphone. Bori was Phillip's closest friend and business partner. The conference call was taking place in Phillip's home office since he had taken the day off to work from home.

Phillip had met Bori in business school during one of the medical technology innovation competitions hosted by the university. They had hit it off and had remained in touch after graduation.

Phillip had gone on to take over his family's business, Dexington Healthcare—a network of hospitals, health plans, medical centers and rehabilitation networks, physician organizations, physician specialty groups, and more recently, a medical device company —a major employer in his city of Dexington. His family had been one of the firsts to arrive at the city many centuries back.

Bori, on the other hand, had headed off to Silicon Valley in California, where he'd started a small medical devices company, which he sold last year for over a billion dollars to a major global medical technology firm. After handing over the reins of his company to the buyer, Bori now spent most of his time speculating in healthcare stocks, monitoring his investments, and looking for the next big idea.

"I'm here," Phillip responded.

"Look, I know you hate the idea of having someone external to the company review the proprietary documents before the product launch. But we need Dr. Greene. Having him—as one of the best orthopedic surgeons in the country—provide an independent opinion on Arthrodev would really help our marketing strategy. You know Arthrodev is a breakthrough product for knee implant surgery and rumors of the product launch have already spread everywhere. A lot of orthopedic surgeons in the area and from out-of-state have committed to coming for the Dexington Medical holiday party. His opinion would mean a lot to these surgeons."

"Bori, having him onboard is not the issue. I'm just hesitant to do that before the launch. We are down to the wire here, and the next few days are critical. I want to minimize the risk of any leakage before the launch given what happened last time."

"Phillip, I get why you're antsy about this. But Dr. Greene has a reputation to protect, and I've worked with him before. You have nothing to worry about from him. We've already advanced beyond the stage we were in when the last incident happened. You have the patent for the device as well as the approval notice from the FDA. The thirty-day waiting period given by the FDA has also ended. The only thing outstanding at this point is the private license, and I've been assured we'll get it in the next day or two. We need to give Arthrodev its best shot, and this arrangement with Dr. Greene will help us towards that goal."

Phillip rubbed his forehead. "I need to think about this."

"Okay, but you have to let me know at the latest two days before the party. He needs a minimum of forty-eight hours before he can commit. The good thing is he is already in Boston for the holidays, so it would be easy for him to come to Dexington."

"I'll think about it and let you know."

"Okay. What about the other preparations for the launch? Are we all set?"

Phillip spun his custom navy-blue leather swivel chair around. "You don't need to ask about it. That's a well-oiled machine. There are committees for committees that are planning the holiday aspect of the party. The strategic planning and marketing team are on top of everything else."

Bori chuckled from the other end of the line. "My bad. I totally forgot. So, speaking of holidays, any plans for Christmas? Are your parents in town?"

"You know them. Always traveling. It's like Mother is trying to make up for all the time that Father had to run the company and was never available. They are in Europe for Christmas. There is some

Russian Opera that is in town that she wants to attend, and some friends they want to meet up with. They won't be back till the New Year. I'll spend Christmas the usual way."

"Why don't you come and hang out with Annie and I for a change? She would love to have you."

"Bori, I have no plans to be a third wheel. And besides, I'll be spending the holiday with the children."

"Listen, Phillip. Your plan for Christmas is all well and good, but you need your own family too. Or we can settle for a girlfriend. Christmas is more fun with a woman you love by your side."

Phillip snorted. "I don't need a girlfriend to have a great Christmas, especially not with the launch around the corner. Besides, nothing beats Christmas with the children at the orphanage, and I always have lots of fun."

"It's not the same, and you know it. Can you imagine Christmas without Annie?"

Phillip smiled. Annie was one special woman. Bori had been lucky to make her his wife. And she practically had Bori wrapped around her little finger, even though Bori would never admit it. He envied their relationship, and it sometimes made him wish he had a special woman of his own. There had only ever been one person that had made his heart skip a beat, but she had disappeared from his life before he'd had a chance. And he'd never seen her again. Even if he met her tomorrow, there was no guarantee she would still be the same kind of person.

The other women who had come and gone since then had only been interested in his money. A few years ago, he'd decided to open his heart to love. But the one relationship he'd taken a chance on had been a mistake he'd regretted. He had shut and locked the door of marriage ever since and thrown away the key.

Phillip sighed. There was no point in dwelling on what would not change. "Annie is special. Good women like Annie are hard to find," he said instead.

"But you need to open your heart and give yourself a chance to find the one. I know Nicole did a number on you, but there are lots of women that are not like her. Anyway, keep an open mind. You never know what would happen. Hold on." Phillip heard voices talking in the background. Then Bori came back on. "I have to go. I'm taking Annie to Napa Valley. I've promised her on my honor that I'm going to relax, which according to Annie's definition means switching off my phone."

The corners of Phillip's lips turned up into a smile. "Is that even possible?"

"Hey, I'm not that bad."

"Yeah, right."

"Contrary to what you think, I can do without my phone. What that means is that I won't be able to talk to you anytime soon, but I'll be back online about three days before the party. Let me know then what you've decided about Dr. Greene."

"Don't worry. I'll be just fine. Have fun with Annie and extend my regards to her."

"Alright, alright, I'll drop the topic. But I want to hear some good news by the time Annie and I get back."

Phillip laughed. "Talk to you later. Merry Christmas."

"Merry Christmas to you too. I gotta go, I can hear Annie calling me. Don't forget what I said!" The line went dead.

Phillip disengaged the speakerphone and leaned back on his chair. Bori meant well, but there was no way he was going to follow his advice. Phillip had been naive before and had been bitten by a snake. That's one mistake he would never make again. And he definitely didn't need a woman to be happy. Unless a miracle happened, Christmas was going to be the same as last year's—a memorable time with the kids.

Phillip checked his watch. It was three p.m. Time to get moving if he was going to be able to buy gifts for the kids at the mall and pick up the Christmas tree on his way to the orphanage.

He grabbed his keys, pulled his credit card and driver's license from his wallet, and tucked them into his pant pocket. There was no need to take his whole wallet since it was just a quick trip and back. Then he picked up his coat from where it rested on the coat stand at the corner of the room.

A knock sounded on his door, and Phillip looked up. The door opened and Geoffrey, his family butler, peeked in. Geoffrey had been with the family for as long as Phillip could remember and was now in his forties. The way his mother told the story, Geoffrey's father had served the family but had died when Geoffrey was still a young boy of fourteen. Geoffrey had then marched straight to his parents and offered to take his father's position. Phillip's father had seen no reason to refuse him and had let him work part-time with the family till he became eighteen.

"Yes, Geoffrey, what is it?"

"I wanted to remind you that it's time, sir." All attempts to get Geoffrey to call Phillip by his first name had failed, so Phillip had stop bothering.

"Thank you." Phillip donned his coat and walked toward the door.

Geoffrey opened the door wide. "Which car would you like to take?" he asked.

"The truck will do just fine."

"You'll find it out front in the driveway."

Phillip held back a chuckle. "You know me so well, Geoffrey. Thank you."

A faint smile hinted at the corners of Geoffrey's mouth before disappearing. "My pleasure, sir. Do you need me to go with you?"

"I'll be just fine. I'll see myself out."

"Very well, sir," Geoffrey said. He turned and strode toward the back of the mansion.

Phillip stepped out of his home office, shut the door behind him, and headed outside.

CHAPTER TWO

Welcome to Dexington. It was emblazoned on a large signboard that pointed toward town. Sarah's heart fluttered as she drove down the road that had branched off the highway. She was finally here. It had seemed like a pipe dream. Only a few days ago, she'd been slaving away at her waitress job in Los Angeles to earn the paycheck that paid off the final loan. And now she was in Dexington, all the way on the east coast.

She hadn't been to this part of the country since she'd left with her family many years ago. And it wasn't like she had a job lined up or lots of family and friends still living in the area. But Dexington had always represented a piece of happiness to her, something that had been dearly lacking in the past few years.

Her parents had divorced not long after they'd moved to California, and it seemed the light in her mom had died with it. She'd refused to work since then, so Sarah had had to work two jobs to make ends meet. She'd turned down her admission at the University of Pittsburgh to major in Finance and had ended up attending a local community college instead. It had taken a miracle for her to graduate, and she'd hoped things would get better.

But then she had met Sean. What should have been a great time of love and dating had spiraled into a nightmare. Her boyfriend had been a wolf in sheep clothing—he'd run up credit card debts in her name and disappeared.

Sean had convinced her mom to sign a credit card authorization form on Sarah's behalf which added Sean to Sarah's account. She didn't know how he'd known her mother could do it. Sarah had been furious with her mom the first time she'd found out she could copy Sarah's signature. Her mom had insisted she wouldn't do it again. It had been devastating to learn she had broken her promise.

She couldn't report the case because an investigation would have been launched, and Sean would have been more than happy to throw her mother under the bus if he was caught. That meant criminal charges against her own mom, something she didn't have the heart for. That left Sarah with no choice but to work three jobs to pay the debts, taking whatever work was available.

She was sure Sean had sweet-talked her mother into it. For some weird reason, her mom had a soft spot for Sean—said he reminded her of Sarah's father though Sarah couldn't see the resemblance.

But it had been hard to look her mom in the face everyday. So as soon as Sarah had paid off the final bill, she'd known it was time to get away. And what better place than the one where she'd recalled spending the happiest times of her life.

Sarah had made the decision in an instant and had taken time off work, packed her bags, and left a note and some money on the table for her mom. She was sure that her mom had seen it by now. Sarah wasn't abandoning her. She just needed time away from her mom to think about her life and experience a bit of happiness again. And Christmas was perfect. It had always been her favorite holiday. She'd hoped to return to this town where she'd first felt the magic of love and Christmas. Maybe, just maybe, her life would brighten again.

Sarah inhaled deeply. Even the air smelled different—free and full of hope. She hadn't thought Betty, her little yellow Volkswagen Beetle, would make the long trip over. They'd been together a long time, and she had felt bad leaving her behind. So she'd driven her all the way—she would decide what to do with her when the time came to leave.

Sarah leaned forward and stared at the houses that flew by. Dexington city was just as quaint and picturesque as she remembered it. She was greeted by various-sized historic country homes on the outskirts which morphed into brick-lined streets and colonial structures that dated back centuries as she drove closer to its main streets. She'd always loved its small town feel, and the springing up of modern buildings here and there had not ruined it. Even the post office with its aging half-brick facade was still in the same spot like she remembered.

Sarah thought about the days ahead, and her shoulders felt lighter like a weight had been lifted.

She drummed her fingers on the steering wheel and hummed a little. She had about a week off to do whatever she wanted. It would be fun to reconnect with her classmates, though she wasn't sure who still remained in the area. Even though a lot of families stayed in Dexington—given that it was a vibrant city —some of the younger folks left for the bigger near-by cities like Boston and New York.

But she still had her one best friend, Veronica. When Sarah had called her once she was on her way, Veronica had squealed on the phone and insisted that Sarah stay with her. Veronica had tried multiple times over the years to get her to visit, but that hadn't been possible with her situation. Sarah was supposed to meet her at the cafe outside the dental office where Veronica worked once she arrived. But she had made good time and gotten to Dexington earlier than planned.

Sarah continued to drum her fingers on the steer-ing wheel. She would visit St. Andrews orphanage instead. She'd spent many good times with Veronica there. The Christmas memories from their time to-gether was the best. And the director was like a sec-ond mother to her. But she could not go empty-handed, and she needed a few supplies for herself as well.

That meant a stop at the local mall. She looked at the portable GPS on her dashboard. The mall was just a mile away and seemed to still be in the same place like she remembered.

She should be in and out of the mall in no time.

Sarah locked her car with a definitive *beep*. She'd been lucky to snag this spot in the mall's parking lot just as the previous car was leaving. Her Californian street savviness had been very handy in maneuvering her car into the space before anyone else, even before the red vehicle she'd spied from the corner of her eye. She tucked her large clutch under her arm and turned to head into the mall, only to see a pair of eyes staring at her from behind dark aviator sunglasses.

Sarah couldn't help appreciating the view in front of her. The owner had a face that could only have been made to torture girls with its handsomeness. He was dressed in a a black military-style jacket, and the grey beanie on his head complemented the five o'clock shadow that graced his angular jawline. His hands rested lightly on the steering wheel as he sat in a red truck that seemed to come from another era.

But wait! Wasn't it the same vehicle she had just outfoxed? No wonder the car looked familiar. And from the position of the truck and its blinking lights, it seemed he had been waiting right there for the spot to open up!

Sarah's heart dropped, and her face grew warm. She had just cut the line! And here she was thinking that she'd arrived at the spot the same time the red vehicle had. Shoot! It wasn't the best first impression. Not that she had any plans to get to know him better, even though he looked delectable.

Sarah felt his continuing gaze, and her heart picked its pace. Wait! Why was he looking at her like she had two heads? It had only been a parking spot and nothing else. Maybe it was just her imagination. She checked behind her to make sure—there was no one there. She touched the corners of her mouth. She wasn't drooling or anything. Interesting. So she was really the star of his show.

But why was he looking at her? She didn't know him—there was no way she would have forgotten a face like that. A tiny voice told her he was probably staring because of the way she had stolen his spot, but she ignored it. As much as she felt bad about grabbing the space, it wasn't really her fault that she had been faster than him.

But for some reason, she couldn't stop looking at him, and her heart accelerated in a familiar way. Not again. The last guy her heart had raced for this way gave her monumental heartache in return. She couldn't let that happen. What if he was just another con artist, or worst case, a serial killer? In her experience and from what she'd read, it was always the nice-looking ones. Her boyfriend had been just as charming, yet he had almost wrecked her life. There was no way she was going down that road again. And the best way to make sure was to prevent him from getting a chance to talk to her. Because she had a weird feeling that was what he planned to do next.

So there was only one action left to take.

Sarah gripped her clutch and hastened toward the mall entrance.

CHAPTER THREE

Phillip looked around. The Prestige Mall parking lot was full, and there was no free spot in sight. He rubbed his forehead and let out a long exhale. There went his dream of being in and out in record time. Why hadn't it occurred to him that it would be this bad? He would have been here much earlier.

He drove quietly around the lot and looked around, hoping another car would leave soon. He'd forgotten that parking space was a premium in Dexington downtown, with the mall being the only place that seemed to have much more than a handful of parking spots. So it was little wonder that it was always packed, and the Christmas season had only made it worse.

Phillip continued to drive around and his eyes swung from left to right as he searched for a spot. But all he saw were shoppers rolling carts piled high with checkout bags, loaded with gifts and holiday decorations that threatened to topple them. Christmas jingle filled the air from the speakers around the mall. There were holiday lights everywhere—from the mall entrance to the top half of the buildings, even to the parking lot light poles. Greeters dressed in cheerful Christmas attire welcomed shoppers to the mall.

After two rotations around the parking lot, Phillip still hadn't found a spot. He sighed. Maybe it was time to leave. He swept his eyes once more over the area, and a movement at the corner of his eye caught his attention. A car was pulling out three rows from the mall entrance!

Wonderful! Phillip drove as fast as was allowed to get close to the spot. Indeed a black Lincoln Navigator was exiting. He idled his truck to wait for the SUV to leave and checked his watch. He still had forty-five minutes. Enough time to get in and out of the mall and still make his appointment.

The sound of squealing tires filled the air, and Phillip looked up. A flash of yellow buzzed past him. A Volkswagen Beetle had come out of nowhere and beat him to the spot!

He clenched his jaw. Didn't the driver know anything about parking lot etiquette? There was no way he or she didn't see him waiting—it seemed the driver needed a good talking to. As he unlocked his truck to get down, the driver's door of the yellow car opened. A young lady clad in black turtleneck with blue skinny jeans and black knee-high boots stepped out, her Californian blond hair in a ponytail. She locked her car and turned; only then did he get a full view of her face.

Phillip's heart almost exploded.

CHAPTER FOUR

Phillip couldn't believe his eyes. It was her. Sarah Nash was here, standing right in front of him!

Even though her hair was no longer its original brunette color and she was much older now, Phillip could still recognize her anywhere. The oval face with its wide expressive eyes, kissable lips, and cheeks that dimpled when she grinned. But she wasn't smiling now and her face looked like it had seen much sorrow. Yet, she was more beautiful than the last time he'd seen her. Before she'd disappeared.

He remembered her: funny, down-to-earth, with

an easy laugh. She had been one of the more popular girls in his class. Yet, she could easily have passed for a nerd—she'd loved numbers and had been proud of it. She probably didn't remember him or their brief encounter many years ago; he'd been one of the quiet ones who hung out at the back of the class. A lot of his classmates had been intimidated by his family's wealth, so he hadn't made much friends. But she'd been nice to everyone and had always said hi to him whenever she saw him. That had gotten him interested in her. So he'd been really upset when he'd arrived in school one day only to learn that she had transferred out, especially after they'd shared a memorable moment the day before. And he hadn't seen her since.

Phillip stared at her and his heart accelerated. What was she doing in Dexington? Not that he minded at all; in fact his Christmas just got a whole lot more interesting. But wait! She was the driver that had just cut in ahead of him and taken his spot. That's what he needed to address now. *Get it together, Phillip,* he told himself. He opened his door to come down and talk to her. That's when he noticed she was practically sprinting into the mall.

Phillip's eyes widened and then the corners of his

lips turned up into a smile. So that's how she wanted to play it. He glanced at her car—he could see the bags in the backseat. So she was planning to stay in town for at least one night which would be more than enough time to track her down if needed. Now that she had appeared before him, he wasn't going to let her get away. But first, the easiest way would be to catch up with her.

"Hey!" he called after her. She didn't even acknowledge him and broke into a run instead.

Phillip couldn't help chuckling and he jumped down from his truck.

Ignoring the loud blare of a car horn behind him, he locked his truck and raced after her.

CHAPTER FIVE

Sarah turned and saw the handsome man racing after her. Her heart pounded against her chest as she pumped her arms and accelerated. This was madness. Why was he chasing her? Why would he come after her for a mere parking spot if something wasn't wrong with him? Which meant her first instincts were right—he was likely a serial killer. Even if he wasn't, he probably had some screws loose.

Just her luck to run into a psychopath, right when she'd been sure she could make a fresh start. She'd thought she'd seen the last of such people in Los

Angeles, where they'd seemed to ooze from every corner. Who would have thought she would find one in Dexington? But if he thought he could catch up to her, he had another thing coming.

She raced into the mall, her eyes darting left then right. The place teemed with people of all ages moving in all directions. Thank goodness she had her favorite cap in her clutch in addition to the sunglasses she always carried—she had picked up the cap from the table when she dropped the note for her mom and had planned to put it in her suitcase later. She pulled the cap out, stuffed her hair into it, and donned the dark glasses. Now he couldn't recognize her so easily. But she still needed to find a place to stay out of sight.

So where was the best place to hide from a madman? Because what else could she call the man who was chasing her? She noticed a maternity shop up ahead on the left. That would work. There was no way he would think she would be in there—she was sure he'd noticed her trim figure.

She hastened into the shop, grabbed an armful of clothing from the racks while ignoring a sales girl that tried to engage her, and headed toward the back where empty stalls waited. She strode into one and locked the door behind her.

Sarah heaved a sigh. She would stay here for as long as needed. Once the coast was clear, she would leave the mall through its second exit and double back to the parking lot to check if his car was still there. If it was gone, then it was likely he had left. She would resume her shopping at that time.

She settled in on the padded chair in the stall to wait.

CHAPTER SIX

Phillip entered the mall and looked around. The intoxicating whiff of sweet pastries filled the air and mingled with the heady overload of bath products, perfumes, candles, and greasy food. Shoppers moved like tightly packed sardines past the storefronts, but Phillip could not spot Sarah's striking blonde hair, despite being head and shoulders above most.

Where could she be? He stepped into the first shop on the left and scanned it quickly. Nope, no Californian blonde hair. He hurried out of the shop and rushed into the second one on the right. She

wasn't there either. It was like, *poof*, she had disappeared. He noticed a maternity shop up ahead, but
there was no way she would have entered the shop.
She hadn't looked pregnant, and there had been no
ring on her finger. Yes, he had checked.

His heart sunk. Where had she gone to? Had it
really been Sarah that he'd seen, or had it just been an
illusion from his wishful thinking earlier today? Good
thing there was one way to confirm it—he had mem-
orized the Beetle's license plate number. Geoffrey
could easily locate her with it if she was still in town.
Phillip had learned over the years that there was no
information Geoffrey couldn't get. How he accomplished it was anyone's guess.

His phone beeped. Phillip pulled it out and
looked at the screen. It was a reminder for his appointment at the orphanage. He pinched the bridge
of his nose and squeezed his eyes shut for a moment.
He would be late if he didn't hurry.

Even though he would have loved to comb
through the mall for her, he had to forget Sarah for
now. It was time to focus on what had brought him
here in the first place—buying Christmas gifts for the
children.

CHAPTER SEVEN

Phillip lifted the little girl above his head as she gingerly placed the silver ornament on the Christmas tree.

"Higher, Uncle Phiyip!" Hanna, a cute four-year-old girl with blonde ringlets that bounced, wriggled in his hands as she placed another ornament on the tree.

Phillip raised her higher. He enjoyed helping the children from the orphanage decorate their Christmas tree each year. He'd picked up the tree from the Christmas farm on the way back from the mall—it had been the largest one available and barely stopped short of the home's living room ceiling. And today had been so much fun. He wished Bori was here to see that the time with the children was so worth it, and not like the dreary Christmas holiday he'd imagined Phillip would have.

The other children had already hung most of the ornaments and decorations that had been collected over the years, their time spent together sweetened by hot chocolate and cookies. Hannah was responsible for making sure that the angel ornaments made it to the top of the tree. Good thing Phillip was tall enough that they hadn't needed a stool.

Hannah giggled as she completed her task, and her laughter soothed his soul. It was at times like this he wished he had a little girl of his own, a girl with dimpled cheeks and long wavy hair that looked so much like her mother's.

Wait! What was he thinking? Phillip shook his head. Just because he had imagined he'd seen Sarah today didn't mean he was already marrying her and having a kid with her. True, he'd liked her years ago, but she might not have liked him back, even with what had happened between them. And what if she was no longer the same person as before, but was now like the other women who flocked after him for his money? People changed all the time, and Sarah could have been no different.

"Uncle Phiyip, I've finished," Hannah's voice interrupted his musings. Phillip looked up at the tree to see that Hannah had placed the final ornament at the top. He set her down gently and tickled her. She giggled again and hurried off through the front door to join the other children playing outside.

Phillip's mouth curved into a smile, his heart warmed by her sunshine. Good thing she was already wearing her coat; the air was nippy enough as it is.

He turned back and studied the Christmas tree—sparkly with ornaments of red, gold, and silver—with blinking tree lights draped around it.

"It's beautiful, isn't it?" a melodic voice said. Phillip turned to see Martha Stockbridge, the director of the orphanage standing beside him. He hadn't heard her come in.

She had been the director of the orphanage for as long as Phillip could remember. A round matronly woman, her formerly long blonde hair was now all white and cut in a short bob. Phillip had met many orphanage directors in the course of his family's charity work, but Martha was different. Her love for the children was never ending. She was probably the main reason why many children who had grown up in the home were doing well in their adult lives— quite a number returned regularly to help with the other children or donated to the home to keep it going. She had truly created a family here.

He beamed at her. "Good afternoon, Ms. Stockbridge," Phillip said.

"Oh stop it, Phillip. You should have gotten used to calling me Martha by now."

Phillip smiled and said nothing. This was one battle she wouldn't win. The habit had been ingrained in him many years ago by his mother.

"Thank you for bringing the tree," she said.

"It was nothing."

Martha's eyes twinkled. "It's never nothing where the children are concerned. This is one of their favorite activities of the season." She patted his arm. "You did good."

They both turned back to the tree and admired it for another minute.

Martha broke the silence. "I think now is a good time for us to wrap the children's presents. Elise," the director gestured through the window to a young woman in her thirties who was chasing the kids in the front yard, "will keep them occupied till it's time for dinner."

"Sounds good to me," Phillip said.

"Oh! And there's someone who will be joining us." The director's face became animated in a way he hadn't seen before.

Interesting. Who could this special person be? "Is it someone I know?" Phillip asked.

"She should be arriving any moment."

Just then Phillip heard loud footsteps climb the front steps and stop in front of the other side of the door. They both turned at the sound.

"I think she's here," the director said and moved closer to the door.

Philip watched the door open. A vision in black turtle neck with long legs clad in dark jeans sailed in. She removed the dark sunglasses she was wearing and smiled at the director.

Phillip's heart skipped a beat. He couldn't believe his fortune.

He didn't need the license plate number anymore.

It was Sarah Nash.

CHAPTER EIGHT

Sarah dropped the bag of gifts for the children on the floor, pulled off her gloves, and rubbed her hands together. She had forgotten how cold Dexington could be. Martha Stockbridge stood in front of her, and Sarah's face broke into a smile.

"Hello, Martha," she said shyly. This was the woman that had been more like a mother to her. The one that had been there all those years whenever Sarah escaped from her house to avoid her parents' fights. And she still looked great after all these years.

Sarah had first met Martha through Veronica.

Veronica had grown up in the orphanage, but you would never have known from the way Martha treated her. Sarah had been envious of their relationship and had been shocked when Martha had also included her as one of her own. She always had cocoa and cookies for them and had listened with a ready ear to all of their girlish chatter and complaints.

They had grown close, and Sarah had stayed in touch even after her family had moved to California. Martha had called Sarah every year at Christmas and on her birthday. She'd always picked up Sarah's call no matter how busy she was and had been there for her when Sean wrecked havoc in her life.

"Come here and give me a hug." Martha rushed toward Sarah with her arms wide open.

As the director's arms settled around her, Sarah could smell the sweet cinnamon scent that was uniquely hers, and she nestled deeper into the hug. She had come home.

"Let me look at you." The director stepped back a bit and appraised her with concern. "You look thin. Have you been eating well?"

Sarah chuckled. Martha had definitely not changed. As far as she was concerned, everybody looked thin and needed extra food.

"Come." The director pulled her along by the hand. "There's someone I'd like you to meet." They stopped short in front of Phillip. "Sarah, meet Phillip. Phillip is one of our regular volunteers here, a wonderful young man who brought us this beautiful Christmas tree you see behind us. Phillip, Sarah is a special daughter after my own heart. She just came in from California."

But Sarah didn't hear the rest of Martha's words. All she could see was a tall handsome young man with gorgeous brown eyes like chocolate pools that drew her in, dressed in an army-green-colored cashmere Henley with dark blue jeans that molded to his frame. This was one handsome dude. As much as Sarah shied away from relationships, she still appreciated a great eye candy when she saw one.

"I believe we've met." His rich voice swirled and tickled her insides as his eyes twinkled with mischief.

Sarah's heart beat faster. "Are you sure?" She couldn't recall seeing this face, though a thought niggled at the back of her mind that she had. But she brushed the thought away. A face this gorgeous could only be memorable.

"You really can't remember?" He shook his head in disbelief at her blank expression. "We met earlier today at the Prestige Mall parking lot."

Parking lot? Sarah's thoughts raced to put the pieces together. She hadn't really met anyone at the mall except … No way, it couldn't be. The psychopath? She peered at him and her face heated. It was really the guy in the vintage truck! He was no longer wearing the beanie and the sunglasses. She had been relieved when she'd discovered that his truck was no longer in the parking lot and never thought she'd see him again.

Sarah felt her neck and ears grow impossibly hot. The director had just called him "wonderful," a term she didn't use lightly. Martha had always been a great judge of character for as long as Sarah could remember. Which meant Sarah had judged him wrongly. This was terrible.

"Parking lot?" The director looked from Sarah to Phillip.

Sarah quickly locked eyes with Phillip and pleaded with him not to tell the director.

A smile tugged at the corners of his lips.

Did this mean he was going to? Or not? She couldn't tell. Sarah waited with bated breath.

He turned to Martha. "I think we should start wrapping the gifts before the kids change their minds and come back in. Where did you say the gifts were?"

Sarah exhaled slowly. *Thank God.*

"This way, in the back room." Martha said. "Come, Sarah. You'll help as well, won't you?"

Sarah picked up her bag of gifts and followed them toward the rear of the ranch style house. "Sure, I'd love to. I brought some gifts for the kids as well. Veronica gave me ideas on what to buy."

"That's so wonderful of you. We'll add them to what we already have."

The director led them to a grey nondescript door. She pushed it open to reveal a mid-sized light-grey-colored room decorated with splashes of purple, orange, and white furnishings. Tall white bookshelves filled with colorful book spines lined one wall. Light from a large window in another corner of the room streamed over two comfortable-looking sofas with a small coffee table nestled between them. Large rolls of Christmas wrapping paper and adhesive tape rested next to a small brown box on the surface of a long desk that hugged the wall opposite the window.

Sarah's feet sunk into the plush dark grey carpet as she walked over to inspect the bookshelves. They were filled with books from literature classics to manga and everything in between.

"What is this room?" Sarah asked.

"It's one we designed for the older children. They'd been requesting a place of their own for quite sometime now, where they could relax without distractions from the younger kids. But this room only became available when we moved everything we had in here into the outside storage we built over the summer. That's when we noticed that it had too nice of a window to let it go to waste. The older kids are pretty excited about it. They'll have access to the room from the New Year, so we've stored the gifts here in the meantime."

"It's nice. I like it," Sarah said.

"Why don't you both grab a seat? The gift items are in those sacks along the wall," Martha said, pointing to a corner of the room.

Sarah's eyes followed to see large white gallon-sized bags that leaned against two of the bookcases. She hadn't noticed them when she inspected the shelves.

"A few more gifts brought in recently are under the desk," Martha continued. "I've attached a sticky note to each present so you'll know who it's for. All you need to do is wrap a gift, write the assigned name on a shipping label with a permanent marker, and then stick it on the wrapped gift. You can find the shipping labels and the markers in that box on the desk." Martha turned to Sarah. "I'm assuming you're all set with the gifts you brought?"

Sarah nodded. Veronica had given her a heads up on how Martha liked the gifts to be wrapped.

"Awesome. We'll catch up later, my dear. It's so good to have you back." Martha gave her another hug.

"It's great to be back too," Sarah said with a smile.

"Okay, I'll leave you guys to it. I still need to make some calls for the Christmas carol night." With that, Martha left the room.

"There's going to be a carol night organized by the orphanage?" Sarah asked Phillip. "There was never one while I was here."

"I think they started it about five years ago, and it has been a hit with the children. Why don't you grab a seat?"

Sarah pulled back one of the black metallic folding chairs leaning against the desk and sat down, placing her bag of gifts on the floor beside her. Phillip did the same and sat down after she did. Interesting. So Phillip was one of those chivalrous types.

"So is the carol night just for the kids?" Sarah asked.

"No, the whole community is invited. All the staff, volunteers, and their families also attend."

"You seem to know a lot about it."

"I've helped organize it a few times."

They settled into the gift wrapping and worked in silence. For some reason, Sarah felt comfortable in his presence, even though she had only known Philip for like two seconds.

She kept sneaking a glance at him whenever she could. The way he furrowed his brow when he was concentrating. The contrast between his solid presence and the careful way he handled the gifts like they were delicate treasures that one couldn't afford to break. This man was an enigma. One she felt a pull to learn more about, even though it probably wasn't a good idea for her.

"So, why did you run earlier?"

Sarah startled. She'd been so engrossed in looking at him that the question caught her by surprise. Hopefully, he hadn't seen her staring. She scrambled for what to say, so she said the first thing that popped into her mind. "I thought you were a serial killer."

Phillip broke into laughter. He even had a nice laugh, one she would love to hear again.

"What made you think so? Do I look like one?" Phillip asked.

"Well, I mean, you were staring at me so hard."

"And you didn't think it could have been because you were pretty?"

Sarah almost choked and she cleared her throat. He thought she was pretty?

He leaned toward her. His spicy woody scent with a hint of citrus-mint enveloped her. Light, not too much, just the way she liked it. "Are you okay? Do you need water?" His eyes flashed with concern.

She waved him away. "I'm fine. It's nothing." She picked up a shipping label and scribbled on it. "I had heard that it's always the nice-looking ones. Serial killers I mean."

"So, I'm nice-looking, eh?"

"Sort of." There was no way she would tell him what she really thought.

She kept her head down and reached for the last gift. Her hand brushed against his as he reached for it as well. A delicious electricity shot through her hand to her whole body. She jerked her hand away, taking the last gift with her. Sarah kept her head down as she wrapped the gift, keenly aware that he was watching her.

"All done," she announced.

"Phew. That's a lot of gifts," Phillip said. "The children will be so happy." He leaned back and cocked his head. "So Miss Sarah, what brings you to Dexington at this time of the year?"

"It's Sarah, thank you." It seemed like he waited for her to say more. But what could she say? That she came on a whim? There was no way she could tell him that.

"I came for a white Christmas, you know, white snow."

He arched an eyebrow. "We haven't had snow during the holidays in a long time. And the forecast never said we would have one."

"Well … And to see some friends. But I'm still hoping and dreaming that snow falls."

"What's so special about the snow?"

"Building snowmen. It's been so long I did that. It's one of my fun memories about Christmas. And the children would enjoy it too. But the best part is drinking hot chocolate on the porch later in the evening while watching the snow fall. Have you ever tried it?"

"No, I haven't. It sounds interesting."

"You should try it sometime."

"I will."

Sarah hadn't expected to talk so much about herself to someone she barely knew. And she didn't want the conversation to drift to what had brought her to town. It was time to change the topic. "Thanks for not telling the director back then about how we met," she said.

"My pleasure. But it means you now owe me."

Was he being serious? It wasn't like she had really done anything wrong, and he'd been the one chasing her. But she had nothing to lose from hearing him out. "What do you want?"

"I'll—"

The door burst open, and they both turned in its direction. It was Martha.

"We have a problem, and we need your help," she said.

CHAPTER NINE

Phillip stood up and pushed back his chair. "What is it? Is everything all right?"

"Elsie just hurt herself chasing the kids. I've had one of the other volunteers take her to the ER," Ms. Stockbridge said.

"Is she going to be okay?"

"She'll be fine. I think she just sprained her ankle, but we can't take any chances," Ms. Stockbridge said. "Now we have a problem. As you know she was supposed to prepare dinner for the kids."

That was true. Elsie was sort of the resident

cook. Phillip had joined the kids a couple of times for dinner at the director's request. "I can make alternate arrangements for their meal," he said.

The director gave him a faint smile. "Thanks for the offer, but there's really no need. The kids want to turn it into a vacation and eat peanut butter and jelly sandwiches. You know Elise is all about making sure they eat their vegetables, so she hardly ever allows them to eat that. I need someone to do a quick grocery run so that we can buy enough supplies to make it for them."

He didn't blame the kids. Elsie had made him eat his vegetables too. "I can get it," Phillip said.

"I'll come with you," Sarah responded.

"Awesome. Here's a card you can charge it to." The director extended the card to Phillip.

There was no way he could take that. He'd had so much fun today with the kids that this would be a small way to say thanks. Phillip pushed her hand back. "There's no need for that. Consider it my treat."

"Thank you," Ms. Stockbridge said.

A loud wail sounded from the front of the house. The director's face creased with concern. "I think I'm needed. Thanks again." She left the room.

"Shall we?" Sarah said.

"Give me one minute to make a call. I'll be right back." Phillip strode from the room and walked down the hallway till he found the nearest bathroom. There was a bucket of water near the sink and some cleaning supplies had been placed beside it. Someone had been ready to clean the room. He pulled his phone from his pocket and called Geoffrey.

"Geoffrey, there is a Miss Elsie from the orphanage that's just gone to our ER. Could you call and make sure they take extra care of her?"

"Yes, sir."

"Thank you, Geoffrey."

Phillip ended the call and tucked the phone back in his pocket. He washed his hands and wiped them dry on a paper towel.

His phone buzzed and a familiar ringtone rang out. It could only be his parents. As he pulled his phone out, he heard a splash sound. What was that? He looked down to see his driver's license and credit card floating in the bucket of water.

"Argh!" How could this happen? He reached down into the bucket, fished them out, and examined them. Good thing they still looked okay. He rinsed the cards off in the sink, wiped them down with a paper towel, and ran them under the dryer. His phone kept ringing in the meantime.

He left the cards under the dryer, pulled his phone out, and pressed its green button. "Hello, Mother."

"Is everything alright? You didn't pick my call on time."

"I was in the middle of something. Is everything okay?"

"We are good. Your father says hello. I just wanted to find out how you are doing. Christmas all alone is no fun."

"I'm good, Mother. I can take care of myself. What's really going on?"

"Nothing, nothing. Your father is driving me crazy. He's been singing all these songs to me all day, and you know how tone deaf he is."

Phillip chuckled. "Tell him to stop."

A sigh came through from the other end of the line. "I can't. He says it's a special Christmas present to me, and he's practiced so hard to make it good."

"Well, enjoy it. Do it for love."

"Speaking of love, I'm hoping you'll introduce a nice girl to us this holiday."

"Mother—"

"It's about time. You need to forget about Nicole."

"Mother, I have to go."

"Son, this isn't the end of this conversation. We'll talk more about this when we get back."

"Bye, Mother."

"Alright. I can hear your Father calling me. Be good, okay?" The line went dead.

Phillip sighed. He loved his mother dearly, but sometimes he wished his parents could just back off his case. He picked up the cards from under the dryer and tucked them into his pant pocket. Was it so bad to just want to be left alone, even though he knew everyone meant well? He didn't need their help.

But Christmas was already looking up since seeing Sarah again. There was no way it was pure coincidence. She was the last person he'd expected back in town, and her effect on him was still the same, even more. Their chat had been fun—now he wanted to spend more time with her. Grocery shopping with her would be a good start. But that didn't mean anything was happening between them. He didn't really know her that well. Too many years had passed. And he wasn't ready for a relationship.

But there was nothing wrong in getting to know

her better. A thought occurred to him, and his lips rose in a lazy smile. The surprise would be perfect. He made another quick call and then tucked his phone back in his pocket.

Phillip exited the bathroom and walked back down the hallway to look for Sarah. She must be wondering what took him so long.

Hopefully, she hadn't left.

● ● —————— ● ●

"That will be three hundred and twenty dollars."

Phillip handed over his card to the cashier and focused on moving the bags of groceries into the cart that Sarah held in place.

"I'm sorry, sir, the card was declined," the cashier said to him.

What was the cashier talking about? There was no way his card could be rejected—it had no limit. "What do you mean declined?" Phillip said. "There must be a mistake. Could you try again?"

The cashier—a young-looking pimply teenager with a Mohawk fade haircut—swiped the card again. "It isn't going through. Do you have another card?"

Phillip winced. This was something he'd never experienced before. This couldn't be happening to him. And not in front of Sarah of all people. He looked behind him and saw that some of the shoppers on the long queue were already growing antsy.

Phillip ran a hand through his hair. Right now, he had only three choices: return all the items, ask Sarah to pay, or give Geoffrey a call to bring a card or cash for him. The third option would take too much time —the children were waiting, and he didn't want to draw any more attention to himself. The other two alternatives would make him look bad in front of Sarah, but that couldn't be helped. The children were counting on him, so returning the groceries was out of the question. That left only one option, even though it left an unpleasant taste in his mouth. But this was a chance to prove what he had always said— he could do anything for the kids.

Phillip swallowed. "Sarah, would you mind paying for the items? There seems to be something wrong with my card, and I didn't bring my wallet."

Sarah said nothing. She pulled some cash from her clutch and handed them over to the cashier.

But if looks could kill, he'd probably be dead by now.

Courtesy of Sarah.

CHAPTER TEN

Sarah stepped down the stairs in front of the ranch house. They had delivered the groceries to the children, and the older kids were making the sandwiches. Martha had asked them to stay for dinner, but Sarah had declined. It had been a long day, and all she wanted to do was go home and rest. She'd called Veronica earlier before going grocery shopping to let her know she'd meet her at her place instead.

Sarah had been shocked at what happened at the store. She'd thought Phillip was different. When she'd interacted with him as they wrapped the gifts, something about him had spoken to her soul. Against her better judgment, she'd been willing to get to know him a little better.

But that had been a mistake. He was just like Sean —another con artist. If he knew he didn't have any money, why had he declined Martha's offer to pay for the groceries? There had been no need to impress anybody, especially not her. And what if she hadn't had enough money to cover the cost? Then the kids would have been disappointed and hungry. Now she was out of three hundred and twenty dollars, money she couldn't afford.

She'd been too angry to speak to him on the ride back. And all she wanted to do right now was get as far away from him as possible. If he thought she was an easy target, then he had another thing coming. Instead of pretending to be who he wasn't, he was better off living within his means—there had been no point in showing off with all the expensive clothes and wristwatch. Yes, she'd noticed it was a designer watch; it practically screamed money. But all that didn't matter to her. She liked a guy who was comfortable with who he was and what he could afford. That's the kind of guy she needed in her life. Not that she'd been thinking of dating him or anything.

It was better to leave now before he came out. She walked to her car, unlocked it, and sat in the driver's seat. She then turned the ignition. No response. She turned it again. Not a peep. *Not now!*

There was a knock on her window. Sarah turned her head to see Phillip standing outside her door. What did *he* want?

"Sarah, is everything okay?" Phillip asked.

Sarah pressed the button to lower her window. "It's fine. The car won't start. It has happened before."

"Can I take a look?"

"There's no need. I'll just keep it here for the night and get a mechanic to take a look at it tomorrow."

"Can I give you a ride home then?"

"No, thanks. I'll just call my friend to pick me up."

"About what happened earlier—"

Sarah waved him away. "It's fine."

"I'll pay you back—"

"You don't have to." Sarah didn't want to have anything to do with him anymore.

"It's not a problem. I'll bring it tomorrow."

"Good night, Phillip."

Phillip studied her for a few moments and then walked away to his truck.

Sarah blew out her cheeks and then picked up her phone to call Veronica. Then she rested her head on the steering wheel and closed her eyes as she waited. Sarah tried not to look in Phillip's direction. She let out a long exhale when she finally heard the sound of his engine turn over as he started the truck and drove away.

Thank goodness he was gone. All she wanted was to have a great Christmas in Dexington.

No other complications, not even Phillip, were welcomed in her life.

● ● —————— ● ●

A loud knock on her window jostled her awake. Sarah turned and saw a figure in a hooded coat.

She screamed, the hair on her skin standing on its ends.

"Open the door, Sarah. It's me, Veronica," a familiar voice said.

Sarah peered closer, and sure enough, it was Veronica staring into the car with her dark brown eyes, her beautiful caramel skin glowing even at night.

Sarah cracked open her door and stepped out. Her exposed face tingled at the sudden change in temperature. "You scared me! I almost had a heart attack!" she said.

Veronica laughed, her voice lyrical in the air. "Sorry. I wanted to have fun at you for a change. Remember how you used to scare me all the time?"

Sarah smiled and grabbed her friend in a bear hug. "It's great to see you."

"I know. It's been too long." Veronica held her at bay and scrutinized her. "The blonde hair suits you, even though I miss your dark wavy hair. All the boys in our class loved your hair."

To Sarah, that was a lifetime ago, and the memories seemed like they belonged to someone else. "You look great."

"You too. I've missed you, my friend." Veronica gave her another hug. "You must be exhausted."

"I am. And Betty won't start."

Veronica glanced at the yellow car as she blew some air into her hands and rubbed them together. "Don't worry, we'll have her checked out tomorrow. In the meantime, let's get your bags into my car."

Sarah looked around for Veronica's car. All she saw was a grey Lexus a few feet from where they stood.

Her eyes widened. "Wait, is that your car?" Sarah walked over to where the car was parked.

"You like?"

"I love! It's really nice." Sarah narrowed her eyes at Veronica. "Why didn't you tell me you bought a new car?" She doubled over as if hurt.

"I'm sorry," Veronica said. "I just didn't want to seem insensitive, given all you had going on."

Sarah straightened back up and beamed her a smile. "Just kidding, ha ha. But don't hold back next time. I need all the good news I can get to give me hope." She walked around the car till she came back to where Veronica stood. "I remember how you always said you would buy a Lexus when you grew up."

"I know. And I was ready to wait till I could afford it, even if it was when I was old and bent." Veronica flashed a mischievous grin. "Luckily, I didn't have to wait *that* long. I scrimped and saved, and then I got lucky. A couple I knew were looking to retire and relocate to Florida and didn't want to take their car along. So I got it for a really good price."

"I'm happy for you, my friend."

"And you've done great too, don't forget that." Seeing the look on Sarah's face, "It's true, even if you don't believe it. Given all you've had to overcome, I must say you've done pretty good."

Sarah let out a nervous laugh. "I still have a long way to go."

"And that's why you are here. To new beginnings!" Veronica pumped her hand in the air.

"To new beginnings!" Sarah echoed. A dog howled back in the background.

They turned at the sound and stared at each other for a moment before bursting into laughter. Sarah felt some of the tension from the day ease away. It'd been a long time since she'd laughed like this. She'd made the right decision in coming here.

"Come on, let's grab your bags before we freeze," Veronica said, looping her arm through Sarah's.

Sarah smiled and allowed herself to be led. This was what she needed. Good honest friendship. Not any man.

And definitely not Phillip.

●• —— •●

"Your place is beautiful," Sarah said touching the plush green and red throw pillows that were cuddle-worthy. The smell of pine and citrus filled the air. "But in the last pictures you sent, your living room colors were cobalt blue, white, and magenta."

Veronica rolled her eyes as she brought in Sarah's final bag. "That was so last season. It's now fall and Christmas time, so I redecorated." At Sarah's pointed look, "Don't worry, it didn't cost me much. I only bought new covers for the couch and pillows. The rest of the furnishings are a basic white, so I can rotate colors easily around them regardless of seasons."

Sarah plopped down on the couch. "I could just stay here forever and never move. That's how tired I am."

Veronica sat down beside her. "I hope the trip was okay."

"It was. I listened to an audiobook for most of the way, so that helped to drive away the boredom. I got in a bit early, so I went to see Martha."

"She'd been so excited that you were coming."

"It was so nice to see her. We didn't get a chance to really catch up. I helped instead in wrapping the gifts."

Veronica looked at her. "That's a lot of gifts. Was there anyone else around to help?"

"Yes, there was a guy named Phillip."

Veronica straightened up. "You met Phillip."

"Yes."

Veronica scratched her head. "Wait. Hold on for one second. What's with the lackluster response?"

Sarah told Veronica what had happened at the grocery store.

Veronica shook her head. "There must be some kind of mistake."

"Definitely no mistake. He's just another con artist."

"Impossible! Unless you are talking about another Phillip. Don't you remember?"

"Remember what?"

Veronica looked at Sarah like she had three horns. "I can't believe this."

"Wait. What's the fuss about?"

"This is Phillip, we are talking about. *The* Phillip. Heir to Dexington Healthcare, the largest hospital system in the area. Hello! The most eligible bachelor in town. And a billionaire to boot."

Sarah almost jumped up from the couch. "What?"

"I'm telling you. Something must have happened to his card. And not everybody is like Sean."

Sarah covered her face with her hands. "What did I do? Just kill me already."

"Hey, what's with the dramatics? Wait! Do you like him?"

"No," Sarah said into her hands. But she could feel her face heating up.

"You're blushing. You do like him."

Sarah grabbed a red throw pillow and buried her face in it.

"Oh, and there's something else."

What could be worse than treating a legit billionaire like he was broke? Sarah peeked out at Veronica with one eye.

"Remember that boy that saved your life at the orphanage many years ago? The one you dreamed about but couldn't remember his name?"

"Yes?"

Veronica leaned back and gave her a pointed look. "Well, that was Phillip."

CHAPTER ELEVEN

Phillip removed the beanie as he entered his house. Geoffrey appeared out of nowhere to take his coat.

"Thanks, Geoffrey," Phillip said as he handed both items over. "The kids all say hi."

"I'm sure they loved the tree," Geoffrey said.

Phillip arched his brow. "How did you know I was buying a Christmas tree? Oh, right, you probably heard from Miss Roth."

Geoffrey's ears reddened. "I don't know what you are talking about, sir."

"Come on, Geoffrey. Everyone knows that you

and Miss Roth are dating. In fact, I can almost bet that she won't be working at the Christmas tree farm by this time next year," Phillip whispered conspiratorially. "She'll probably be a fixture in this house by then."

Geoffrey battled to hold back the smile that tugged at the corners of his lips. "I don't know what you are talking about," he insisted. "Would there be anything else?"

"I'm good. Good night, Geoffrey."

"Good night, sir."

Phillip walked beyond the foyer to a panel on the wall and pressed it. A door opened on the right to reveal an elevator. He entered and rode it to the third floor, where the doors slid open to reveal his fifteen thousand square feet apartment with its fourteen-inch floor-to-ceiling windows that provided a beautiful view of the city. He padded across the luxurious ankle-deep carpet to his walk-in closet that was large enough to equal any average-sized home in Dexington. There were sections for his suits, shirts, sweaters, jeans, and adjustable racks for shoes and man-purses. A ginormous central island with built-in velvet-lined drawers served as the focal point of the closet, with its see-through glass-top displaying numerous ties, belts, wristwatches, and cuff-links.

Phillip removed his Vacheron Constantin wrist-watch and custom-designed belt and placed them in separate drawers. He strode out of his closet into his living space and collapsed on the custom oversized Italian leather couch.

He mentally kicked himself. How could he have made such a mistake—running the card under the dryer? Of course he'd been told that neither a dip in water or drying could destroy the chip card, but a little risk from heat damage had still been there. He should have anticipated that and had a new card delivered at the entrance of the grocery store.

Philip sighed. There was no point in beating himself up about a situation he couldn't turn back. Geoffrey would get a new card for him in the morning.

He thought about Sarah. It had been embarrassing to ask her to pay. There was no way he wasn't going to return the money back to her, no matter what she'd said.

Phillip crossed his legs. But why had she become so aloof after the incident? It wasn't something to be happy about, but her reaction had seemed extreme.

He rubbed his eyebrow. Did it mean she was the kind of lady who was crazy over money? If it was true, that would be disappointing. It also meant he had to be careful. He'd been down this road before and didn't need that kind of woman in his life, no matter how much he was attracted to her. And from the way Sarah had spoken to him in the parking lot, it seemed she had made up her mind about him.

Phillip closed his eyes and let out a long exhale. Maybe he was lonely and didn't know it, which was why he had allowed himself to be carried away with her. It was probably best to forget what might have been.

His thoughts turned to the children at the orphanage, and his face relaxed into a smile. He'd received a confirmatory call on his way home that everything was ready for their surprise. And for her if she showed up.

He was certain they would love it.

CHAPTER TWELVE

Sarah opened her eyes and groaned. Even though she'd slept through the night, her head felt like it was going to split into two. And her nose was all stuffy. All the traveling must have done her in. Because it was just plain wrong to get sick during Christmas time.

Sarah remembered her conversation with Veronica last night, and she buried her face into her pillow. She'd misjudged Phillip and had treated him badly. She'd allowed her fear of someone like Sean getting close to her again override her objectivity. And she had hurt Phillip in the process. She'd been so sure he was not who he projected himself to be.

And to make matters worse, he was the boy who had saved her, the boy she'd had a crush on. She hadn't gotten his name that night when everything happened, so she hadn't known it was Phillip. And he'd only been a boy then, very different from the man he had become.

When would she learn that not everyone was like Sean? She banged her head against the pillow but got the headboard instead. Ouch!

Sarah rubbed the tender spot. The only way to make it right would be to apologize to him. To be honest, Sarah would have preferred to crawl into a hole first. She wasn't ready yet. But if she didn't get it over with, it would become harder to do so later. She would have to put on her big girl pants and do the right thing. But it didn't have to be today; she had to be clear-headed for Operation Apologize-to-Phillip.

She dragged herself out of the queen-sized bed and shuffled out of the room in her pajamas into the living space. It had an open floor plan, and the kitchen was awash with light from its large windows.

Sarah looked around. Where was Veronica? She was supposed to be off work today. She noticed a large covered plate on the marble kitchen countertop with a note on top of it. The enticing aroma emanating from it made her stomach growl.

Sarah walked over, picked up the note, and scanned its contents. Veronica had left coffee for her in the coffeemaker with bacon, eggs, and pancakes in the covered dish. Awesome. But Veronica had gotten an urgent call from work and had to go in. So she needed Sarah to go to the orphanage on her behalf—something about building snowmen with the children.

Snowmen? With no snow? How's that supposed to happen? Veronica must be mistaken. Sarah walked back to her room and picked up her phone from the bedside table. She called Veronica, but it went to voicemail. She dropped her phone on the table and headed for the kitchen again. After pouring some coffee for herself, she sat on one of the kitchen bar stools and took a sip.

It had been a long time since she'd built a snowman; the last one had been in Dexington many years ago. Come to think of it, it was really sad that she had no fun memories of Christmas in all the years she'd spent in California. Building a snowman again would be nice.

But was there really snow? Maybe it was some kind of inside joke. Well, the only way to confirm was to go to the orphanage and see for herself. It would be a real tragedy if it was true, and she'd missed out.

Sarah rubbed her temples. Time to take a pain reliever and pray that her stuffy nose didn't get worse.

And maybe, just maybe, she wouldn't run into Phillip while she was there.

It would be too embarrassing.

● • —— • ●

The taxi dropped Sarah in front of the orphanage. It was already mid-morning and the sun was high in the sky. Dexington was one of those places where it could be cold and sunny at the same time.

Sarah looked to her right and saw Betty parked forlorn in the farthest spot. Veronica had returned her call as she was getting dressed to let her know that she'd had a guy look over Betty. He'd confirmed that she needed new parts, which wouldn't be available in the auto store until after Christmas. So Sarah would have to depend on Veronica or on taxis to get around till then.

Her shoulders slumped. Another expense she

couldn't afford. When would they ever end? She sighed. But there was nothing she could do. She and Betty had come a long way, and she couldn't abandon her.

As she turned to head inside, a familiar red truck passed by and packed in one of the available spaces. Sarah's heart sank. She couldn't pretend she hadn't seen Phillip. Which meant she had no choice but to apologize now. At least her head didn't hurt as much anymore, and she was dressed in passable jeans, her favorite pink cashmere sweater, and a cream winter jacket. Looking good while doing so could only help. She kicked her booted toe against the lowest front stair and waited for him to walk over.

That five o'clock shadow. Sarah had never been a fan of bearded guys until she'd met Phillip. He wore it well, and her heart skipped a beat every few seconds just looking at him. He was dressed in a black turtleneck and blue jeans with a long light-grey coat complemented by a black and white preppy muffler slung around his neck. His chestnut hair had this careless look that became him and made her want to run her hands through it.

She took a deep breath as he came within a few feet. "Hello, Phillip."

"Hi, Sarah." His voice was cool.

Sarah almost lost her courage. "I'm so sorry about yesterday," she said. She rubbed the back of her neck. "I shouldn't have been so cold to you."

His eyes assessed hers. "I tried to tell you what happened."

"And I should have listened and not cut you off."

"When I left you yesterday after the gift wrapping to make a phone call, my card fell into a bucket of water, and it didn't occur to me it might have been damaged during the process of drying it. That's probably why it didn't work at the store."

Sarah felt like a fool. "I'm sorry. I should have given you the benefit of the doubt," she said quietly.

"Why didn't you?" he asked, his eyes intent on her.

Sarah's hand played with the collar of her coat, and she looked around. Only she and Phillip were in the parking lot. Good. She didn't need anyone else knowing the story of her life. She turned her eyes back to him. "I had someone who did the same thing, who eventually took advantage of me and wrecked havoc in my life. So the incident yesterday reminded me of that. I was afraid you would do the same. I'm sorry."

Phillip shifted his stance. "I'm sorry that happened to you, and I should have gotten an alternate card immediately." He dipped his hand into his pocket to pull out his wallet, opened it, and slipped out three hundred dollar bills and a twenty. "Here's the money. I should pay you back."

"No, don't—"

He took her hand and placed the money in it, folding her fingers over it. "I would feel better if you took it," he said. "I was the one who promised to pay for the groceries."

"Okay." She really did need the money especially with Betty's expenses.

But he didn't let go of her hand. And his hand fit so well over hers like a glove. She didn't want to let go, but the truth was that she didn't belong with him. As much as she had confirmed he wasn't like Sean, she had too much baggage to let someone else into her life.

She slipped her hand slowly out of his. He looked at her, his eyes expecting more. "Can we be friends now?" he asked.

Her lips twitched in a smile. "Maybe."

"Uncle Phiyip!" Sarah turned to see a little girl racing at full speed toward Phillip. He picked her up, lifted her, and twirled her around. Her giggles filled the air. Gosh, he was such a natural with kids. Who would have thought? The other children surrounded them, and one started pulling Sarah's hand. "Come and help us build snowmen," they cried.

Snowmen? There was snow? Sarah gave Phillip a questioning look, but he only smiled in return and allowed the children to pull him toward the backyard.

Sarah followed along with quickened steps.

She had to see this miracle for herself.

CHAPTER THIRTEEN

"We are going to split into two groups," one of the older girls said. "The boys in one group, and the girls in another. The group that builds the biggest snow-man wins." All the children nodded their agreement.

Sarah's mouth had fallen open on seeing the snow. It was piled high and filled every corner of the backyard. It hadn't snowed in Dexington yesterday or today, so this much snow was a total mystery. And the kids didn't know how it had gotten here. All they remembered was waking up and looking outside the window only to see it. Even the director and the other staff had no idea what happened.

But she wouldn't look a gift horse in the mouth. Building a snowman during the Christmas holidays was a dream come true for her. And the weather was perfect—not too cold but with clear skies. She'd better enjoy it before the snow eventually became slushy and melted away.

"Are we ready?" Sarah asked.

"It's on," Phillip responded with a twinkle in his eye.

Sarah smiled. If he thought she would lose, he was in for a surprise. She turned to the girls. "We'll win, won't we, girls?"

"Yes!" the girls responded enthusiastically.

"Boys, let's show them how it's done," Phillip said. The boys hollered in response.

"Wait!" a little voice chirped. It was Hannah. She squinted up at Sarah. "Sorry, Miss Sarah, but I'm going to join Uncle Phiyip." The other girls snickered and teased her about being a sellout. Phillip shrugged and mouthed, "It's my charming nature."

Sarah rolled her eyes, but a smile spread on her face once she turned her back to him.

She clapped her hands together. The girls quietened down. "Okay, girls, let's do this." She led them back to the section of the backyard they had previously claimed as their own, next to an ATV, and began to direct them on the art of building a formidable snowman.

● ● ——— ● ●

"We won!" The girls high-fived each other. Sarah stuck out her tongue at Phillip before turning back to the girls. She'd won against him! Her insides quivered with excitement.

A large cold weight landed on her back. What was that? She craned her neck backwards to see what had happened. Someone had thrown a snowball at her! She looked in the direction of where it had come from and saw Phillip grinning at her.

Really? Two could play this game. Sarah bent down and scooped some snow which she balled in her hands and threw at him. It landed right on his face which made all the children laugh. Sarah couldn't help but giggle. He looked ridiculous with the snow running down his face. He quickly wiped it off with his hands, molded a snow ball, and threw it at her. The snow fight was on.

All Sarah remembered of the next few minutes was snow flying in the air in all directions, children

running around and shrieking with joy, and the feel
of cold snow hitting her body as she ran to dodge
the snow balls. She laughed so hard that she almost
peed her pants. It was a glorious feeling, one she
wanted to treasure and never let go. Even her
headache had disappeared, and her nose didn't feel
stuffy anymore.

She saw Phillip from the corner of her eye sneaking to hide away among the trees that lined the back
of the property.

Like she was going to let that happen. She molded the biggest ball she could make and threw it at
him. It landed in the center of his face, and he went
down and stayed still.

What had she done? She hurried to where he lay
and bent beside him. "Are you okay?" Her eyes
looked for signs that he was alright. He opened his
eyes at that moment and held hers. Everything else
faded, and the air between them crackled with energy.

Sarah couldn't move—it was like his gaze held
her captive. Her heart beat faster, and her face grew
warm. Her breath hitched. The more she looked at
him, the more it felt like she could see into his soul,
into the core of who he really was. And in that moment, something changed between them—like they

had crossed a threshold.

It was suddenly too much for her. If she didn't pull away, she would literally drown in his eyes. And she wasn't sure what would happen next. But whatever it was, she wasn't ready for it.

Knowing she would probably regret what she was about to do, Sarah forced herself to break eye contact with him. Unsure of what to do with herself, she sat on her haunches and brushed snow off her jacket.

"Everyone, come on in! Time for hot cocoa!" Martha shouted through an opened back door. By this time, Phillip was sitting up.

"Time to go in," Sarah said, avoiding Phillip's eyes.

She stood up and headed into the house without waiting for his response.

CHAPTER FOURTEEN

Sarah sat on a chair on the back porch and sipped her cup of hot cocoa. She looked at the sky—its colors were muted as the sun sunk lower, casting dark shadows on the trees that lined the property. She hadn't planned to stay the whole day, but it had ended up that way. They had played board games with the children, and it had been so much fun. Just like she'd hoped her family would have done in the past. Before she knew it, it was already evening.

She could hear the children's laughter behind her as they watched some TV show. This was life the way she had always longed for—peace, serenity, and lots of laughter. A sense of unhurriedness. It was something that had been missing in her life for a long time.

Sarah took another sip of her drink. If only she could bottle up this moment and take a whiff of it whenever life became too much for her. Because this wasn't permanent. She would be a fool to think otherwise. And of course, she couldn't deny that the presence of a certain somebody definitely made it more enjoyable.

Phillip. No matter how much she denied it, she felt something whenever she was around him, something she hadn't felt with Sean. There was a certain frankness about him, like he'd opened himself up for her to read like a book. An earnestness for her to truly get to know the real him. And it didn't help that he was handsome enough to eat. But that wasn't the best part about him.

He'd been the boy who saved her. That put him in another league altogether. What he had done many years ago was a sacrifice not many people could make, only by those who truly cared about others more than themselves.

She heard the door creak open behind her, and

she sensed his presence even before she saw him. He settled into the chair next to hers. They stayed silent that way for a while, sipping their cups of cocoa, and enjoying the sounds around them. She closed her eyes and sighed with pleasure.

"Are you okay?" he asked, his soothing voice reaching into her and curling around her heart. Somehow, it felt okay to reveal a bit of herself, to be vulnerable with him.

"Yes, I'm just happy. It's been a long time since I had this." She swept her arm in front of her. "Peace, laughter, calmness."

He didn't say a word and waited. Like this time belonged to her, and he didn't wish to intrude. Sarah opened her heart a little more.

"Thank you for saving my life many years ago."

"So you do remember me. I thought you had forgotten," he said.

"I didn't. I mean I did." She threw up her hand. "Oh, what am I saying?"

He chuckled. "Take your time."

Sarah took a deep breath and let it out. She placed her mug on the floor beside her feet. "I remember a boy that saved me, but I had no idea it was you, and I didn't know your name. You look different though." At his arched brow, "More yummy."

Phillip burst out in laughter.

Sarah threw her hands over her face. "Did I just say that? Oh, stop laughing!"

"Okay, okay, I'll stop," he said with a tease in his voice.

Sarah stared out at the beautiful landscape for a moment. "Why didn't you tell me you were the one who saved me?" she asked finally.

"I thought you would remember."

"I didn't even know it was you. It was my friend Veronica who reminded me last night. Do you remember her?"

"Of course. You were like two peas in a pod. You went everywhere together. And I'd met her a couple of times here at the orphanage."

She cast a curious glance at him. "How did you know we were always together?"

"She didn't tell you? We were all in the same class."

Sarah gasped. "Really? I don't remember you."

"That's because I was always sitting at the back and was never into the same groups or activities like you. And I used to wear glasses too."

Sarah clapped her hands together. "Now I remember you. You were the class nerd!"

"Ouch!"

"No, seriously, I liked you then. You were quiet, but you had a certain confidence about you that I admired. But I knew then that we weren't in the same league."

He leaned toward her. "You liked me? What about now?" His low baritone voice washed over her and drew her in.

Her heart raced into a gallop. She swallowed. "Uhm."

"Are you saying you don't like me anymore?"

"That's not what—"

"So you do like me?"

"Well …" What was wrong with her? It wasn't like a cat got her tongue.

"Sarah …" The sound of her name on his tongue sent thrills through her. Oh, man! Phillip was killing her, and she could feel her resolve melting away. She had to get things back on track.

She got up and leaned against the porch post. "You know, I don't really recollect all that happened that night."

"What do you remember?"

"I left my parents' house that evening after they

had started fighting as usual. It was the Christmas holidays, and you would think they would set their differences aside for a while. The fighting became too much, and I had to get out of there." Sarah could sense Phillip now standing beside her, but she chose not to look at him. "I got on the bike and headed down to the orphanage. The main road was slippery, so I decided to take an unfamiliar shortcut I had seen the other children from the orphanage use.

"I rode my bike as fast as I could. It was like I couldn't stop hearing my parents' voices, and I wanted to get away from it all. I reached the orphanage's side gate, but then forgot there was a small pond very close to it. It had frozen over, and I wasn't looking. The next thing I knew, my bike slipped. I fell off, cracked the frozen surface, and went down into the iced water." Sarah had not talked about this part of the incident since it happened. But somehow, she felt comfortable sharing it with Phillip.

"It was like nothing I had ever experienced before," Sarah continued. "I felt like I was outside my body, watching myself go down this watery grave, knowing I would never be able to come out again. A part of me wanted to let everything go, but another part wanted to live—that someday down the road, my life would be much better, and everything that had happened would become history.

"That's when I felt strong arms lift me and I hung on for dear life. Then I became sleepy; it was like my body was trying to shut down, and there was nothing I could do to stop it. But then I heard your voice say, 'Sarah, don't fall asleep. Fight it!' I knew I had to give it everything I had. And then we were out.

"I couldn't stop shaking, and you wrapped your arms around me to warm me up. Which totally doesn't make sense to me now since we were both as wet as could be. But it was one of the best feelings in the world at that time. I needed that. A hug from someone who cared enough to risk his life for me." Sarah looked at him. "You could have died, you know, in that pond. But yet you jumped in."

Sarah felt his hand encircle hers, and she leaned against him. It felt good to have finally said out loud what had happened that year.

"I had come with my parents to visit the orphan-age," Philip said. "I'd been bored out of my mind with all the discussions. The children were playing games in one of the rooms, and I didn't want to intrude. So I slipped outside to see if there was any-thing more interesting. I had just stepped out when I heard a breaking sound and then saw a splash as you disappeared through the cracks.

"I ran as fast as I could till I reached the frozen pond. That's when I saw your yellow bike with the funny stickers. I would have recognize that bike any-where; I'd seen you ride it to and from school. All that was in my mind at that time was to save you. So, I jumped in. Luckily, I was able to pull you out. But you were shivering, and your lips were turning blue. I couldn't take off your clothes because it would be improper. So, I did the only thing I knew. I hugged you and gave you CPR."

Sarah turned and punched his arm with her other hand. "That wasn't CPR, that was a kiss, dummy. I know the difference between the two."

"Well, it was CPR. You turned it into a kiss." She could hear the laughter in his voice. And she knew it was true. She buried her face on his shoulder in em-barrassment. "But I didn't mind. I thought it was a pretty great way to end a horrible experience. And that's how the adults found us when they came out."

"Including Martha?"

"Including her and my parents."

Sarah's face grew warm. "Martha never told me."

"I think she was just happy that you were alive.

That was all that mattered. Someone had called 9-1-1, and they sent us to the hospital in two separate vehicles. And that was the last time I saw you till you appeared yesterday."

Sarah glanced at Phillip before continuing. "I was told I slept for two days straight." Sarah said. "After I got better, I told Veronica I wanted to see you again. I asked her for your name, but my parents walked in then. They insisted that Veronica leave; that it was all her fault that I fell into the pond—because I went looking for her.

"At that time, I didn't know my father had been transferred to Los Angeles by his office. My mom had refused to go with him initially. That's what they had been arguing about that night. But after what happened, she figured the best way to get me away from Veronica was for us to go with my dad. They got me discharged immediately, arranged a quick school transfer for me, and we moved cross country a few days later. My mother blocked every effort I made to see Veronica before we left. We lost contact for a couple of years, but a chance connection on social media brought her back into my life. And we've never talked about what happened that night."

"I was away from school for a couple of days

too," Phillip said as he stroked his thumb against the back of Sarah's fingers, his spicy woody scent doing a number on her nerve endings. "Imagine my shock when I went back and heard that you had transferred out." He gave her a mischievous grin. "It was like you stole my first kiss and then ran away. I looked for you, but there was no information on your whereabouts. Even the director and Veronica had no idea. And I was too embarrassed to ask my parents for help. So I eventually gave up."

Sarah felt her insides warm up. He had cared and had looked for her all those first years in California when she'd felt no one gave a hoot about her. "I'm sorry," she said.

"I'm just joking. It wasn't your fault."

She stayed silent. It had felt good to be in his arms years ago. Was it odd that she wished for that hug again?

As if he knew what she was thinking, she felt a hand turn her toward him. "I missed you, Sarah Nash."

Sarah's heart melted and warm butterflies fluttered in her belly.

"Is it okay if I hug you?" he asked.

She couldn't speak and only nodded her head. His

arms encircled her and drew her in.

What Sarah felt next could only be described with one word—home. A place where she belonged. This was what she had missed for a long time. All the weight slipped away from her shoulders. She couldn't help but let out a small sigh. Phillip tightened his arms around her, and they stayed that way.

Then Sarah felt something light land on her shoulder followed by another. She looked up only to see snow flakes falling from the sky.

She gasped. It was magical. Here she was in his arms with snow falling around her. It was the stuff of dreams. And she wished it would never end.

Sarah remained in his arms for a few more minutes. She could have stayed that way forever, but it was getting very dark, and she still had to catch a cab.

She broke contact first. "I need to go. It's late."

"Can I give you a ride?" Phillip asked.

The question was music to Sarah's ears. She hadn't dared to hope for it. "If it's not too much trouble."

Phillip smiled. "It would be my pleasure. Let's go inside and say our goodbyes."

● • —— • ●

"Sarah, it was great spending time with you today," Martha said as she hugged her. "Will we see you tomorrow?"

"I think I'll just sleep in till later in the day. I had a headache and stuffy nose this morning, and I think it's my body telling me that I need some rest. But I'll be at the carol service. I wouldn't miss it for all the world." She beamed at the children. They grinned back.

The director gave her another hug. "Please take as much rest as you need." And then she said more quietly, "And give your heart a chance." Before Sarah could ask her what she'd meant, Martha had already moved away to help a child who had hurt her knee.

Sarah headed toward the door and then turned as she remembered something. "I think you need to cover the ATV outside. It's still snowing," she said to the director.

Martha gave her a quizzical look. "What snow? It hasn't snowed today," she said.

"But ..." Sarah looked at Phillip for confirmation.

Her eyes widened, and her heart warmed with an unfamiliar feeling. The grin on his face told her everything, as the memory of yesterday's conversation came to mind.

He had done it. Made snow fall.

Just for her.

CHAPTER FIFTEEN

Phillip led Sarah to his truck as she buttoned up her coat. Tonight had been unexpected but wonderful. He'd come today ready to forget about her, but she'd been quick to apologize and had opened up to him instead. Building the snowmen with her and the children had been fun, but the snowball fight had been the best. Now he knew what he had missed growing up. All because of her.

He'd sensed when things had changed. They had both known at that moment that it would never be the same again between them. For someone who hadn't wanted a relationship, he'd quickly become open to exploring the possibility of one with her. He liked what he had seen so far, and he wanted to get to know her more. He wasn't sure how long she would be in town for, but it looked like she'd be here till after Christmas. Phillip determined he would make the best use of the time they had together.

He sensed she was probably still reeling from the shock that he'd arranged the snow to make her wish come true. That was one of the perks of having unlimited finances, and for that he was grateful.

Phillip opened the passenger door for her to step in before striding over to his side and getting in as well. A quick question about Veronica's address confirmed which roads he needed to take.

"So, how did you do it?" Sarah asked.

Ah, the question he'd been anticipating. He feigned ignorance instead. "Do what?" Phillip kept his eyes on the road as he drove out of the parking lot.

"Make snow fall from the sky."

He flashed a grin at her. "It's a secret."

"I guess that means you were also responsible for the snow in the backyard."

He said nothing. She probably knew the answer

to that as well.

"Thank you," she said.

It was a word so simple but yet so weighted. Philip's chest expanded with joy. "You're welcome," he replied.

They rode along in companionable silence.

"I'm sorry I threw the first snow ball at you. I didn't know you had a headache," Phillip said, breaking the silence.

"No worries. I had a great time." Her hand played with the collar of her coat. It was one of those cute things he'd noticed she did when she was a little nervous. "So what's up with the vintage truck?"

"It was my father's and his father's before him. I'd always wanted it since when I was a boy, but my father finally gave it to me as a birthday present when I turned eighteen. You don't like it?"

"I think it's cute."

Phillip laughed heartily. "I'm sure Harry is flabbergasted. Calling him cute is a new one."

"Whose Harry?" Then her eyes lit up with understanding. "You mean this truck? I can't believe you name your car too."

"Of course you have to name them. Each one has its own unique personality."

Sarah touched the dashboard. "Harry, I'm sorry I said you were cute." Before she could help it, a giggle escaped from her. And then it turned into laughter. Phillip couldn't help but join in. He liked seeing this side of her.

When the laughter died down, Phillip stole occasional glances at Sarah. He felt more attracted to her than he had in the past. Who was she now? He wanted to know more. "When we were in high school, what did you want to be when you grew up?" he asked.

Sarah shifted in her seat. "I love non-profits, and I wanted to work in Finance. So I thought helping a non-profit manage its investments would be the best of both worlds for me."

He glanced at her. "So did you?"

Sarah crossed and uncrossed her legs. "Well, I passed some of the required certifications."

"Is that all you ever wanted?"

Sarah stayed quiet for a moment. Then she said, "It might sound silly to you, but I've always wanted to ring the opening or closing bell at the New York Stock Exchange. It's something I've always loved seeing on TV. What about you?"

It occurred to Phillip that no one had ever bothered to ask him what he wanted to do. Everyone had always assumed he would take over the family business; they considered any other interests hobbies at most. And he did love his work, but he enjoyed inventing more. Sarah had been the first to ask him.

"I've always wanted to create new tools to make people's lives better," he said.

"Did you?"

He stared into the distance before answering. "Well, let's say my first attempt failed."

"You should try again."

Phillip gave her a quick look. "Why do you say that?"

"Because you have what it takes." At his pointed stare, "I saw the improvements you made at the orphanage. They were simple, minimalistic, but got the job done. It's your dream. You should never let go of it."

Before Phillip could respond, his phone rang. He took a quick look at the screen. It was Bori. "Sorry I need to take this call," he said as he put on his earpiece and pressed the answer button. "Bori."

"Hey, Phillip. I just got a call from one of the FDA Investigators. They need us to resend the engineering studies document. I know we submitted it, but they can't find it in their files. He needs it before they can send the license."

"How is that possible? There's no way we would have received the approval notice without it." Phillip noticed Sarah was staring at him, and he winked at her. She blushed and looked away.

"I agree, and luckily the guy had seen it before, so he knows it was already factored into the decision-making process. We have to get it to them ASAP. I have a weird feeling that Chester Harrison's fingerprints are all over this. I heard he's been sniffing around. We need to seal this before he creates another loophole."

Phillip's fists tightened around the steering wheel, and he fought the anger that threatened to coil up within him. Not Chester Harrison again. He could not let Harrison best him this time around. "I'll head to the house now and send it to you and the FDA in a few minutes."

"Okay, call me when it's done." The line disconnected.

"Sorry about that," he said to Sarah.

"No worries. Is everything okay?" Her blue-gray eyes lit up with concern.

"I need to make a quick detour home before

dropping you off. Do you mind? It will only take a few minutes."

He saw her pulling at her collar again. "That's fine."

Phillip smiled. She had nothing to fear from him. He would never take advantage of her or any lady for that matter. He would make the stop as quick as possible before taking her home.

Phillip made a U-turn at the next light and headed to the wealthier area of the city.

CHAPTER SIXTEEN

Sarah didn't know whether to breathe in or exhale. They had passed through massive wrought iron gates with an intricate leaf design that had opened of their own accord and had approached the stately brick mansion through a long winding road—hedged on either side by beautiful manicured gardens—that ended as a circular driveway in front of the home. A fountain gurgled at the center of the driveway, spraying water from an angel's jar into the pool beneath it. The house was breathtaking, and the largest one that Sarah had ever seen.

As Philip stopped the truck at the top of the driveway, a middle-aged man in a crisp suit and bow-tie appeared out of nowhere and opened the door for her. "Good evening, miss," he said.

Sarah looked from him to Phillip. Phillip has a valet at his house? By now, Phillip had stepped out of the truck, so Sarah did the same.

"Good evening," she responded with a nervous smile as she smoothened down her coat.

"My name is Geoffrey, and I'm the butler. Welcome to Dexington House."

"It's alright, Geoffrey. I'll take it from here," Phillip said.

Geoffrey stepped aside, and Phillip led Sarah into the house.

Sarah's heart almost stopped. She rubbed her eyes to be sure she wasn't dreaming. Phillip lived here? She glanced at him, but Phillip didn't seem to notice her surprise as he guided her further into the home.

They stepped through a cavernous foyer that opened into a large living room. The space seemed to be the center of the home with its ornate carved fireplace, mosaic-tile floors, a central winding stair-case that led to the upper floors, large windows that graced its walls, and sets of french doors that led to other parts of the home. It was stunning and had probably been designed by a talented interior designer. Sarah felt out of place in such a beautiful home with her twenty-five dollar cashmere sweater that she'd snagged in a sale.

"You can have a seat here." Phillip pointed to an oversized cream sofa that was so pristine that Sarah hesitated to sit down. "Give me a few minutes. I'll be right back."

He walked down the hallway to the right of the staircase and disappeared through a set of French double doors.

"Would you care for orange juice, miss?" a voice said from her right side.

Sarah almost jumped from her seat. How had Geoffrey appeared beside her without her noticing?

She gave him a tentative smile. "Thank you." She grabbed the drink from the tray and took a long gulp. The sound echoed in the air and Sarah's face grew warm. "Sorry, I was thirsty."

Geoffrey's expression didn't change. "No worries, miss. Is there anything else I can do for you?"

"Could you please call me Sarah?"

Geoffrey gave her a curt nod. "Yes, Miss Sarah."

Sarah almost burst out laughing. It seemed Geoffrey was incorrigible. She settled for a smile. "Can you please tell me where the bathroom is?"

"Please, follow me." He dropped the tray on one of the side stools and led Sarah to a white door that stopped short of the double doors. "This way." He opened the door for her.

She stepped in and gasped. The powder room was luxurious and feminine and had definitely seen a woman's touch. It featured a delicate pink floral wall design and a large marble-topped double vanity that matched the marble mosaic floor. A large arched window framed by long drapery that hung from a high ceiling brought in natural light. A chandelier finished the stunning effect.

Sarah used the bathroom and stepped out. She looked around but didn't see anyone. She heard Phillip's voice from beyond the double doors and she moved toward it and peeked through.

There was a large door on the right that was partly open. Sarah could see Phillip pacing in the room as he spoke to someone on the phone. Most likely the person he had talked to on their way over. Sarah's eyes swung to the left side. There was another door that was partly open that boasted rows and rows of books on massive bookshelves. It was probably the library. It wouldn't hurt to take a look.

Sarah stepped through the French doors and entered the room on the left. It was bigger than she'd thought with its extensive floor-to-ceiling book-shelves. Her footfalls—as she walked up to the shelves and ran her hand on the book spines—were swallowed by the luxurious grey carpet that lined the room. She recognized some of the book titles—they were most likely first editions and a collector's dream. She'd never seen so much, all in one place.

A piece of white paper with colored markings caught her eye on the massive desk toward the back of the room. Sarah stepped to the table, lifted the paper, and studied it. It seemed to be a blueprint of some sort. She peered closer at the document. Most likely a device, but she didn't understand the mark-ings on it.

"What are you doing?" a familiar voice boomed angrily behind her.

CHAPTER SEVENTEEN

Sarah started, and the document slipped from her hands onto the desk. She turned to see Phillip behind her, his face a mask of fury.

"I believe I asked you a question. What are you doing here?" His eyes were now a pair of slits that bore into her.

Sarah swallowed. Why was he so angry? "I …"

"What were you searching for? Who sent you?"

Surely, he didn't mean what she thought he was inferring. "What are you talking about?"

Phillip walked around to his desk and Sarah's eyes

followed him. "How much did they pay you to come and snoop around here?" he asked.

His words rankled her and she squared her shoulders. What gave him the right to accuse her? Did he think she was a thief? "Listen, I was just curious and saw the door open. I spied the bookshelves and thought it was a library. As I was checking out the books, these colored markings caught my eye!" Sarah ran a hand against her hair. "I don't even know what this is," she said gesturing at the markings.

Phillip placed his hands on the document, and his eyes searched her face. "You really don't know?"

"I don't. What is it?"

"It's the blueprint for my latest invention that's launching in a few days." Phillip picked up the paper and rolled it up.

Sarah now understood why he'd been so angry. But that didn't give him the right to blame her. "But why did you leave it out in the open since it was obviously important?"

He placed the rolled blueprint into one of the desk drawers and locked it before answering. "I needed it for the phone call I was making." He gave her a pointed look. "Besides you are not supposed to be in here."

"True."

Phillip came around the desk and leaned against it. His nearness made Sarah's heart race and she caught a whiff of his scent. "I'm sorry I was so mad at you," he said in a quiet voice. "The last invention I had was stolen by someone close to me before its launch and sold to my competitor who then released it. I sued him and ended up in a long and expensive court battle which I eventually won, but he'd already made a lot of money from it before the final court decision came through. And tonight I just got the news that he is sniffing around again and—"

"You can't have it repeat itself," Sarah finished.

Phillip nodded.

In that moment, Sarah saw Phillip's vulnerability. She could imagine how he must have felt to have someone steal something so precious—Sean had done the same thing to her. She longed to make him feel better.

"I had something similar happen to me," she said.

Phillip looked at her. "You did?"

"My ex-boyfriend, Sean. He stole my credit information or more like my mom gave it to him."

Phillip folded his arms around his chest. "What do you mean?"

"My mom is great at copying my signatures no matter what I change it to. Sean convinced her that he needed a credit card on my account, and she signed the authorization form for him. He then proceeded to run up the card and acquire massive debts in my name."

Sarah could feel Phillip's eyes on her. She couldn't look at him—she didn't want his pity.

"Did you report him?" he asked.

"I couldn't. If I did, my mother would have to face criminal charges, and I couldn't do that to her. Sean would make sure he didn't go down alone and would point the finger at her." She drew in a shaky breath. "So I ended up paying off all the loans. There were times when I wanted to give up, but I told myself each time that it would soon be over. It took a few years and working three jobs, but I finally did it. But my heart could no longer bear the knowledge that the people who were supposed to love me were the ones killing me. I needed to get away, and that's why I came to Dexington."

"Come here." Phillip reached for Sarah and pulled her to him. His arms enveloped her, and he rubbed her back. That simple action broke the dam within her, the one that had held tight even when she'd found out the truth about Sean, confronted her mom, and worked hard to pay off the debt.

Sarah sobbed, her insides emptying out all she had held back over the years.

"Ssh. It's going to be okay," Phillip murmured as he continued to hold her in his arms.

The sobs eventually subsided. Sarah let out an exhale and leaned against him. It felt good to finally let everything out. But why was Phillip able to help her in ways no one else had been able to?

She leaned away from him and smiled at him through eyes filled with unshed tears. "I'm sorry for crying. I mean, here I was trying to encourage you, and you end up consoling me instead."

"I'm glad I could help."

"Thanks for listening and for not judging."

Phillip smiled at her. "How could I? All I see is someone who was brave, determined, hardworking, and loyal. I think a cup of hot chocolate and freshly baked cookies are in order."

Sarah laughed. She had been worried what he'd think of her once he found out the truth, but it seemed it had been for nothing.

And in that moment, Sarah realized one thing, the truth that her heart already knew, but she'd been afraid to face.

This man was special, and she had fallen for him.

CHAPTER EIGHTEEN

Sarah woke up and stretched. She'd had a fun dream where she'd had chocolate and cookies with Phillip. They had laughed together a lot, exchanged phone numbers, he'd dropped her at home, and then promised to pick her up in the morning. Oh wait, it wasn't a dream!

Sarah's face split into a grin. It had been a while since she'd been this happy. And she prayed it would last. She'd smiled so much last night once she'd gotten home that Veronica had asked if she was okay. Sarah was floating on the clouds, and she didn't plan on landing anytime soon.

Phillip had said he would pick her up at seven a.m. She looked at the time on her phone. It was six-fifteen.

"Oh shoot!" Sarah jumped out of bed. If she didn't hurry into the shower, she would be late. And she hadn't even picked out what she would wear. "Veronica, I need your help!" she called out as she raced into the bathroom.

Fifteen minutes later, Sarah was all dressed. Thankfully, working three jobs had taught her how to get ready quickly. And Veronica had helped straighten her hair into a sleek ponytail. She was glad she'd done her roots before her trip to Dexington. She looked down at her pink and white dress. It would have to do. He hadn't exactly told her where they would be going, and this was the best that she'd had in her bags.

The doorbell rang throughout the apartment. Could it be Phillip already? "I'll get it," Sarah called out. She hurried to the door and opened it. Her eyes widened when she saw Geoffrey standing on the other side of the door, holding a garment bag and a shopping bag together in one hand.

"Good morning, Miss Sarah."

"Good morning, Geoffrey. It's Sarah."

"Mr. Dexington asked me to give these to you." Geoffrey held out the bags.

"What is it?"

"He didn't say. There is a note in the shopping bag."

Sarah took the bags from him. Geoffrey turned and started down the front stairs.

"Wait!" she called out. Geoffrey turned and looked at her.

"How may I help you, Miss Sarah?" he asked.

Sarah forgot what she had wanted to say. She could be muddleheaded sometimes. "Never mind. Thank you for bringing this."

"You're welcome," Geoffrey responded. Sarah watched as he entered a black Range Rover SUV parked in front of the apartment and drove off.

She stepped back inside and locked the front door.

"Who was it?" Veronica asked as she towel-dried her hair. She was getting ready for work.

"That was Geoffrey, Phillip's butler."

"Butler? Ooh, fancy! What did he say?"

"He just brought me this from Phillip." Sarah showed her the bags. "He said there was a note inside."

"So what are you waiting for? Open it up, let's see."

Sarah laid the garment bag on the couch and zipped it open. There lay the most stylish royal-blue double breasted coat dress that she had ever seen.

Veronica fingered the sleeve. "This is so nice and soft. and the color totally goes with your eyes. And it looks like it's your size. How did he know?"

Sarah opened the shopping bag. There was a pair of black leather pumps, black tights, and a navy square clutch to match. The pumps were also her shoe size. Really, how did he know? She pulled out the card and flipped it open.

Please do me the honor of wearing these.

I'll be at your door at seven a.m.

Thanks,

Phillip

"Now these are adorable!" Veronica peered over her shoulder to look at the note. "What did he say?"

Sarah handed her the note and turned back to the items. They were lovely, but she didn't want them. What she was wearing should work. She didn't need a man buying stuff for her.

"I know that look," Veronica said as she dropped

the note on the coffee table.

"What look?"

"The look that says I don't need these things."

Sarah sighed. "You know me too well."

Veronica took her by the shoulders. "Sarah, where did you say you guys were going again?"

"I don't know. He said it would be a surprise."

"Exactly. Would you prefer to arrive at your destination and find out you were not dressed for the part? It's okay to accept something like this. Maybe when you see him you can tell him you don't like to accept these kinds of gifts. But right now, I give you permission to enjoy being pampered."

Sarah laughed. "You give me permission? I don't recall you ever being my mother."

Veronica gave her a hug. "Enjoy being with a good man for a change. Now go get ready before he gets here!"

"Where did you say we were going again?" Sarah asked as she sat in Phillip's car. He had picked her up at seven a.m. as promised. The streets were practically empty at this hour.

"It's a surprise. Don't worry, you'll love it. Have I

told you that you look nice?" Phillip said, smiling at her as he drove toward downtown.

Sarah's face grew warm. "Like the third time."

"It's not my fault. You are too beautiful for words."

Sarah covered her face with her hands. "Oh stop it, Phillip. And you look nice too." Phillip was dressed in a navy blue dress suit paired with an immaculate white shirt and what looked like diamond-crusted cuff links, all beneath a grey winter coat.

"Thank you."

"And I like your car too." The insignia on the silver and navy blue car had said Bugatti Chiron, but all Sarah knew was that it was a beauty. "What's its name?"

"Charlie."

"Hmmm, nice name." Sarah caressed the dash-board. "Charlie, you are one sexy car."

Phillip burst out laughing. "Hey, what about me?"

Sarah tried to hold back her smile. "You're cute."

"I'm cute? Nothing else?"

Sarah's lips turned up in a smile. She tapped the dashboard with her fingers instead.

"Sarah Nash, I'll get payback for this. Hang on."

Sarah let out a yelp as Phillip accelerated.

●● —— ●●

"Why are we here?" Sarah asked. They had arrived at the underground parking lot of Dexington Health-care and had taken a special elevator to the rooftop.

"You'll see. I'm glad you have your hair in a pony-tail."

"Why?"

Phillip opened the door to the rooftop. A huge helicopter lounged on a helipad with a pilot in the front cabin.

"Oh, wow. This is huge," Sarah said. She didn't know much about helicopters, but it was obvious this was well-maintained. Its surface gleamed, and its rotors looked sharp enough to slice through anything.

The pilot stepped down from the helicopter and ambled toward them.

"Sarah, meet Steve. Steve is my main pilot and takes me wherever I need to go."

"Nice to meet you, Sarah. Have you flown in a helicopter before?" Steve asked.

Sarah looked at Phillip. "No."

"Then you are in for a ride," Steve responded. "It will be fun, but safety will always come first. Why don't we get you all strapped in, and then we can head out to New York?"

Sarah's eyes searched Phillip's face. "New York?"

"That's the beginning of the surprise," Phillip replied with a smile. "Let's go."

The helicopter ride felt surreal. One minute Sarah was all strapped in the back seat with Phillip beside her, the next minute she was up in the air flying over Boston and headed toward New York. The takeoff had been like ascending a glass elevator.

"Are you having fun?" She heard Phillip's voice through the headset over her ears.

Sarah bobbed her head. "I feel like I'm dreaming. Pinch me. Ouch! Phillip, I didn't mean literally." She rubbed the tender spot.

"Let me make it better." He held her hand and caressed the back. His touch sent tiny sparks of delicious electricity down her arm.

"This is really nice. Thank you."

"The ride or the hand?"

"Wait. What?" She smacked his hand.

"Ouch! That hurts."

"That will teach you to be serious."

"Okay, I'm glad you like it. The ride, I mean. We'll be in Manhattan in about an hour. So relax and enjoy the sights."

Sarah looked out the window. It was a perfect day to fly. Though the air was a bit chilly, the sky was clear with minimal wind.

In less than an hour, Sarah could tell when they flew over Central Park. The magnificent view over the lush park was unbelievable.

"Phillip, we have clearance to land in Central Park," Steve said. They made an exception for us."

"Great." Phillip responded as the Belvedere Castle came into view.

"Wow! A castle in New York?" Was this real? Sarah leaned closer to the window. "I didn't know New York had one."

"The Belvedere Castle was designed in 1869 by one of the co-creators of Central Park. It is currently being used both as an observation deck for the National Weather Service and as a New York tourist site."

"It's beautiful," Sarah said. It truly was.

Steve flew the helicopter till it was right over the front grounds of the castle, and then he landed it. Sarah waited till the rotors stopped turning before she unlatched her safety harness. Phillip jumped down first and then helped her down.

She looked around. "But I don't see any tourists."

"The castle is closed for a week for renovations," Phillip said. "But I called in a favor and here we are. This way."

Sarah followed him into the castle and up a flight of stairs till they got to the terrace.

Her mouth fell open in shock.

CHAPTER NINETEEN

Phillip grinned at the expression on her face. This was what he had hoped for. It made arranging it all worth it.

"I can't—"

"Take a deep breath, Sarah."

She inhaled and exhaled. "Breakfast on the terrace of a castle served by a Michelin three-starred chef? The same one I've only seen on TV and in magazines? I don't know what to say."

"Come and take a seat." Phillip led her by the hand to the round table covered with white fine linen tablecloth with two chairs facing each other. Phillip pulled out a chair for her, and Sarah sat down.

Sarah looked around as though searching for something.

"What is it?" Phillip asked as he sat down. "Is there anything you need?"

"This place feels warm. I would have expected it to be chilly since we're outside."

"Oh! I had them warm the space up. We can't have you freeze, can we?"

The smile she gave him told how much she appreciated it.

"Would you like tea or coffee, ma'am?" A young man of about twenty in a waiter's uniform appeared at their table and asked.

"Tea, please."

Phillip cocked one eyebrow. "I wouldn't have pegged you as a tea drinker."

"I drink coffee occasionally, but I'm not really into it. It's a bit too addictive for my taste."

"Same here. I know I didn't ask, but do you have any food allergies? I had assumed you didn't. If my memory serves me right, you loved to taste everything in the school cafeteria."

"Hey, are you calling me a foodie? Which by the

way is actually a good thing," Sarah said. "I just have an appreciation for excellent food. You are right, no allergies here. I'm good with whatever food *he* prepares."

Phillip laughed. Sarah was seriously starstruck. He loved her exuberance.

Phillip nodded at the chef who strode over.

"Welcome to Breakfast at Belvedere. My name is Chef Daniel, and I'll be your chef for today."

Phillip could see that Sarah was trying to contain her excitement, but her eyes betrayed her. Philip hid his smile. He could watch her all day.

"You have the choice of an omelette with smoked salmon and caviar, classic scrambled eggs with European white truffle, or an avocado toast sandwich topped with fresh greens drizzled with jalapeños vinaigrette and pumpkin seed oil," the chef said.

"Hmmm, they all sound yummy. Can I have a bit of each?"

"Certainly. Of course, we'll end with dessert: fresh cake octagons topped with yogurt, berries, and a side of chocolate-strawberry macaroons."

Sarah's smile grew wider. She probably hadn't expected dessert for breakfast.

The chef snapped his finger and the service began.

Phillip smiled as Sarah tucked in yet another bite of food into her mouth. He'd never known eating could be so inspiring—he was full just by watching her eat. He liked her this way, better than all the ladies he'd met in the past, who barely ate a thing. It was obvious she thought the omelette and the scrambled eggs were divine, but the avocado sandwich was her favorite. And he agreed. It had the right amount of spice and tang. She was probably satiated but still managed to eat some bites of the dessert.

"I can't eat anymore." Sarah placed her cutlery on her plate. "I'll never be able to get up from here if I do." She turned to the chef. "This was absolutely delicious. Thank you." She clasped her hands together and gave him a slight bow of her head. The chef smiled and reciprocated in return.

Phillip wiped his mouth with a napkin and placed it on the table. First mission accomplished. "Now that we are done with breakfast, let's get to the real reason why we came to New York this early," he said.

CHAPTER TWENTY

Sarah bit her lower lip. "Phillip, are you sure this is okay?"

"You'll be fine." They stood in the Welcome room of the New York Stock Exchange where the logo for A Wish for Kids was prominently displayed. When she'd mentioned ringing the opening bell as one of her lifetime wishes, she hadn't expected Phillip would make it come true.

Sarah fingered the collar of her coat dress. "Are you sure? We are talking live television here. She suddenly felt nauseous. "I think I'm about to puke."

She placed a hand over her mouth.

Phillip rubbed her back. "Take nice deep breaths, Sarah. I'm right here."

Sarah obeyed. A moment later, she could feel the queasiness subsiding. The back rub helped a lot. "I think I'm better now." She gave Phillip a small smile. "Could you tell me more about A Wish for Kids foundation? I've only heard a little bit about it."

"A Wish for Kids foundation is one dedicated to making the wishes of children all over the US come true." A man in a sharp grey three-piece suit came into view with a stunning woman in a power red suit in tow.

"Hello, Connor, Elizabeth." Phillip said. "Sarah, meet Connor, the President of A Wish for Kids foundation. Elizabeth heads the Investment Committee on the Board of Trustees. Sarah Nash is a friend of mine."

"Phillip, great to see you, man." He turned to Sarah and shook her hand. "Nice to meet you, Sarah. You look lovely."

Sarah's cheeks grew warm. "Thank you." She shook hands with Elizabeth as well. Elizabeth gave a quiet smile in return. Sarah turned back to Connor. "So you were saying about the foundation?"

"A group of friends got together ten years ago and decided to form a foundation that would grant wishes to children in the US," Connor continued. Sarah could tell this was a favorite question for him. "Especially for children either with long-standing illnesses or with a shortened life span from various diseases.

"Making their wish come true could be as small as getting them the puppy of their choice, to as much as flying them and their parents to a safari in Africa. It has grown to be successful over the years, making dreams come true for over ten thousand children.

"Today marks our ten-year anniversary, which we are celebrating here by ringing the opening bell at the NYSE. We hope it would also provide more visibility to the foundation, which could lead to gaining new donors." Connor turned as the door opened and a tall man stepped in, followed by a large group of people. "I think we are about to get started. And the rest of our team is here."

What followed next was a blur for Sarah. The tall man introduced himself as Jim, welcomed the group to the NYSE, talked both about the histories of NYSE and A Wish for Kids Foundation, and congratulated them on the anniversary. The man gave the floor to Connor, who then spoke on the accomplishments of the foundation. It was so much to take in, but Sarah loved every minute of it.

Jim then led the group to the trading floor where many TV media were roaming and reporting. Sarah felt like she was in a dream. So this was how everything looked up close.

The group split into two at that point and a select few, Phillip and Sarah included, proceeded to the platform which overlooked the entire trading floor, and where the opening bell ceremony would take place. Jim explained that since it was the opening session, only the bell will be rung; the gavel was used in addition during the closing bell ceremony.

Phillip's hand remained at Sarah's back most of the time. It helped ground her, and she was grateful for it. This man was really in tune with what she needed.

A Senior NYSE official explained to Connor when he expected him to ring the bell, while the rest of the group took selfies to commemorate the occasion. Sarah was surprised to see Phillip take a selfie of both of them together as well.

Thirty seconds before the opening bell at nine-thirty a.m., the group was instructed to start clapping, and it grew louder as the traders joined them. Connor was given the signal, and he pressed the button like his life depended on it! Sarah clapped as loudly as the others and even gave a large whoop at the end.

A ginormous screen displayed the ceremony, and Sarah couldn't recognize herself on it. The woman on the screen was happy, bright, and beautiful, unlike who she had been for as long as she could remember. She liked the new woman a lot. The whole experience was magical, a moment in her life history she would never forget.

And it was all due to the wonderful man standing right there, in that moment, beside her.

● ● ——— ● ●

The happy group chatted as they walked down the NYSE hallway. The opening bell ceremony had been a resounding success. Phillip held Sarah's hand as he talked with Elizabeth on some of their recent investment strategies. She loved the feel of her hand in his, and her heart swelled with pride that she understood their conversation, despite her limited hands-on investment experience.

But she was amazed at the breadth of Phillip's knowledge. With the way he spoke, one would think he ran a hedge fund as well.

As they neared the exit, Sarah glanced to the right and saw three men standing in front of an open door. Their heads turned in Sarah's direction at the sound of the approaching group, and in that moment, Sarah saw him.

Her heart stopped, and she couldn't move.

"Sarah, are you okay?" Phillip asked.

Sarah's heart picked its speed and pounded against her ribcage. How was this possible? What was he, of all people, doing here? She had to find a place to hide before he saw her.

Still gripping Phillip's hand, she turned in the opposite direction and began to head back down the hallway. Her eyes darted to the left and the right.

She heard Phillip as if from afar tell Connor and Elizabeth that he would catch up with them later.

"Sarah, what's wrong?" Phillip asked.

She couldn't speak. All that consumed her was finding a good spot to stow away. Phillip must have sensed something was wrong because he tried to match her quick steps. A few doors down, she spotted a conference room on the right. A young lady in a service uniform rolled a cart filled with bottles of water to the entrance of the room and then stepped away to take a call. It was the perfect opportunity. Sarah hurried down and slipped into the room, dragging Phillip along.

Her frantic eyes swept across the room. It was barely set up, but there was a covered table in the left corner. It would do. She raced to it, lifted a corner of the table cloth and slipped beneath, pulling Phillip under the table with her.

"Sarah, what's going on?" he asked.

Sarah could hear loud voices outside the room, including the one that used to terrorize her dreams. Her breath came in quick gulps.

"Sarah—"

"Ssh, they'll hear you!"

The door opened and that one voice rose above the others.

Sarah's heart increased its tempo and sweat broke out on her forehead. She just needed a moment for the men to go away, and then it would be alright.

Phillip lowered his voice. "Sarah, why are we hiding?"

She had to do something drastic to keep Phillip quiet before he gave their position away. She had to shut him up.

She pulled him to her and lowered her lips on his.

●● ● ——— ●●

The sounds faded all around her. At that moment, Sarah forgot about the men, about NYSE, and about the fact that they were under a table. All she knew was that she wanted more. She deepened the kiss.

A pain shot through the middle of her head. Ouch! She had hit her head under the table. She broke away and rubbed her hand on the tender spot. Her face grew warm at what she'd just done. "I'm sorry. I need to leave ..."

She made to go, but a hand drew her back in, and then Phillip was kissing her.

Sarah had been kissed many times before, but now she knew those didn't qualify. This, right here, was how a woman should be kissed. A soft tender kiss that drew her in delicately like she was a jewel to be treasured, promising hope, desire, and love. The wonderful feeling of his arms around her, and the way his breath caressed her cheek. It was like all the hurt and stress melted away, leaving behind only sweetness and warmth. At that moment Sarah was lost and didn't want to be found.

Then Phillip pulled away and ran his hand through his hair. "We shouldn't be doing this," he said in a shaky voice.

CHAPTER TWENTY-ONE

Phillip couldn't believe what he had just done. He should have known better than to kiss a woman under the table. But he hadn't been able to help himself. Her lips had called to him ever since he'd met her, and when she had kissed him, he'd only wanted more.

But then he'd remembered the vow he had made to himself. Phillip had decided after the disastrous relationship with Nicole that he would only kiss a woman that he had decided to marry, a woman with no secrets from him. Finding out about Nicole had almost destroyed him, and he wasn't willing to go through it again. And Sarah clearly had big secrets she hadn't shared with him. If not, why had she been frightened, with them ending up under the table?

Who was the man that she had seen and was running from? What did she have to do with him? As much as his heart came alive whenever he saw her, and her little quirks made him smile, and he seemed to forget himself around her, he couldn't disregard what he had seen and needed to protect his heart until he was sure.

But by pulling away, he had hurt her. He could feel her withdrawing from him to shield herself, but there was nothing he could do to stop it.

"Come on, let's get out of here," he simply said.

CHAPTER TWENTY-TWO

What was Phillip thinking? Sarah's heart squeezed in pain that he had pushed her away. She sensed he'd wanted to know what had happened. He should have just asked her, instead of saying nothing and pulling away.

Tucker. Sean's invasion in her life had brought him. Tucker was a loan shark who disguised his business as a debt collection agency. He had purchased some of the loans that Sean had racked up and had personally pursued her to pay back the money. His interest rates on the debt had been high, and Sarah had tried to pay off the loans one after the other, but Tucker had not been impressed.

Instead, he'd harassed her. He had appeared at her different workplaces, which made her change jobs frequently and had even showed up at random times around her home.

But that was not all. The leering and lewd comments had been the worst. But she hadn't been able to report him for harassment. That would have brought the cops' attention to her mom, who would have become entangled in a criminal case, which Sarah would also have been expected to deal with. It had been much simpler to just endure the harassment. She'd thought she'd seen the last of him after paying everything off. But today had proved her wrong.

She shouldn't have run. She didn't owe him anymore. But she hadn't wanted him to meet Phillip, to enter into her new life and pollute it with his vileness. Most people only saw a handsome businessman with a crooked nose. But Sarah knew better. He would invade her life like cancer and would be difficult to cut out.

Sarah tried to banish thoughts of Tucker away. Even thinking about him now was letting him win.

And she didn't deserve that. Neither did Phillip.

But seeing Tucker had reminded Sarah that she was not good enough for Phillip. They lived in two very different worlds. It would be difficult for him to accept her past and her background.

And she wasn't even qualified to stand around him. She had barely managed to get her degree. She had gone to lots of night school which had helped her pass some of her certifications, but she had never been able to keep a steady job. Sarah couldn't blame him if he didn't want to have anything to do with her. Maybe she should just stick with her original plan—enjoy Christmas again in Dexington and leave love out of the equation.

She could accept today for what it was, a special gift and nothing else.

She resolved to enjoy her time with Phillip as long as she could but not expect more out of it.

CHAPTER TWENTY-THREE

The rest of the time spent in New York had been uneventful. Phillip had chatted with Connor and Elizabeth, and then they had all taken some pictures outside to commemorate the occasion. They'd even stayed to watch the replay of the event on the large screens in Times Square, after which Connor and Elizabeth had left for a business meeting, while Phillip and Sarah had headed back to Dexington.

The flight had been short, and soon they were driving on the streets of Dexington in silence. Sarah stole glances at Phillip, but she couldn't tell what was on his mind. Was he still thinking about what had happened earlier? He didn't look angry or anything. She closed her eyes and leaned back into the passenger seat. Or was he just exhausted? He must have had less sleep than she'd had to arrange today's event at such short notice.

"Are you tired?" Phillip's voice broke through her thoughts.

She looked at him. "Why do you ask?"

"I was wondering whether you would be interested in a trip down memory lane with me."

Sarah sat up. "What do you mean?"

"How about a quick look around the class in our old high school?"

Sarah gave Phillip a quizzical look. Why would he be interested in that? High school was like a lifetime ago, and she was sure the school had changed. Well, she had nothing to lose, and no plans for the afternoon.

"Sure," Sarah said. "Any special reasons?"

"I figured since you haven't been back for a while, you might like to see it."

"Oh! Okay, let's go. But won't the school be closed?"

He gave her a small smile. "Don't worry. Leave

that to me."

Sarah leaned back and stared ahead. The billion-aire lifestyle was sure fun—everything one wanted could become a reality.

●• —— •●

Sarah looked around the class. It was familiar but yet different. The wall paint color had changed from cream to a very pale blue, and there seemed to be a few more desks than before. She walked over to where hers had been positioned and examined the desk placed there. It was still the same one! Who would have thought? She had carved her name into the desk at the time. Sarah ran her fingers through the faint grooves that still remained.

She turned to see Phillip in front of what she assumed was his old desk. Now, she remembered him more clearly. He had worn a pair of owl glasses that had looked at odds with the symmetry of his face. She remembered thinking at that time that he would probably be more handsome without it.

And she'd been right. Even as he bent over the desk, the reflection of the sunlight against his hair cast a bronze tint to his hair strands and softened his features. The tightening of his arm muscles evident through his white shirt as he leaned over, indicated a body that was at one with exercise. He'd ditched his coat and jacket as soon as they had entered the school. Not that she minded. She couldn't seem to get enough of looking at him.

And then there was the five o'clock shadow along his jawline. How could one person alone have all this handsomeness? Before she could avert her eyes, Phillip turned at that moment and flashed her a smile.

Sarah almost had a heart attack. Butterflies rose and settled in her stomach, and all she wanted to do was run into his arms. And then she remembered their first kiss many years ago, and the one they had shared earlier. Her face grew warm and she averted her eyes. She would have loved to kiss him again, but that wasn't the kind of relationship they had. He had pushed her away. Probably because so much had changed between them. Her heart squeezed in pain at what might have been between them if she'd never moved to California.

She let out a heavy sigh. There was no point in thinking about the past.

"What's wrong?" he asked, concern written all over his face as he walked over.

"Nothing." There was no way she would tell him what she was really thinking. It would be too embarrassing!

"I see you found your old desk." He hopped on the next one.

Sarah leaned against the edge of hers. "Yes, I did. And it still has my name etched on it. It feels like many worlds ago." A memory came unbidden to her. "Do you remember Mrs. Hutchins?"

"Sure, I remember her. Long beaked nose that moved anytime she spoke."

Sarah laughed and smacked him on the arm. "You're horrible." She sat on the desk. "She was one of the people that really made a difference in my life."

"Seriously? She was always all over the place. Dropping stuff, wearing the wrong colored socks on the other foot …"

Sarah giggled and smacked his arm again. "Stop it. She was comfortable and happy with who she was despite her clumsiness, and always had a nice word for me. Everybody around me only saw the happy cheerful girl, but she knew the real me. She was the first person who saw me crying after my parents had a huge fight. And she just sat there with me and said nothing. And that was what I needed at the time. And the best part? She never mentioned it again. She always had a quick word of encouragement and gave me a card every Christmas. So I was sad when Veronica told me she passed away last year. I never got a chance to thank her for what she did for me."

"You could write her a letter. I'm sure her kids would be happy to see a note about how special their mom was."

"You know, I might just do that. But I don't have her address."

"You can give it to me. I'll make sure it gets delivered. I'm sure there's paper and a pen somewhere around here." He jumped down from the desk. "Let me see." He walked to the teacher's table, pulled the in-built drawer open, and rifled through it. "Aha!" He held up a small notebook he'd found. "I think this should work." He tore off a sheet and replaced the book in the drawer. He walked back to where his jacket rested and retrieved a custom crafted fountain pen from the inside pocket. "And here's a pen. You're all set."

Sarah walked over and grabbed both items from him. "Thank you," she said.

"My pleasure."

She strolled back to her old desk and sat down to write the note. She penned the letter carefully and then folded it before handing it and the pen back to Phillip. Phillip tucked them inside his jacket pocket. "I'll make sure it goes out sometime today."

"Thanks. You know, I now remember how you were back then," Sarah said.

"Really? How so?" By now, he had perched back on the desk he'd been sitting on.

"The owl glasses."

Phillip groaned. "I mean, how could that be the first thing you remembered?"

Sarah shrugged and leaned back in the chair. "It was cute. And you weren't wearing it that night at the orphanage. That's why I didn't recognize you."

"I should have ditched it a long time ago."

"I'm glad you didn't. It made you look approachable. That's why I liked you then."

"You liked me?" A smile teased at the corners of his lips. "Now, the secrets spill. Tell me more."

Sarah hid a smile. "I mean, I liked you as a friend."

Phillip jumped down from the desk. "A friend. A regular friend or a potential boyfriend?"

"Regular, silly."

Phillip held his chest as if in pain. "Ouch! That hurts."

Sarah laughed. "Well, I wasn't thinking about boyfriends at the time." At Phillip's raised eyebrow, "I mean I talked about it a lot with Veronica, but I wasn't ready for one."

"Until you kissed me."

Sarah covered her face. "You are killing me! Could you please stop saying that? I only responded to the nice CPR that I was getting."

"Since I'm killing you and you are dying, would you like another CPR?" By now, Phillip was so close to her, and his woodsy-mint scent was making the butterflies in her stomach come alive.

Sarah wanted his kisses so bad. She still felt the tingle on her lips from earlier today and remembered how the kiss had made her feel. But he had pushed her away at the end. She didn't want to get hurt again.

"No thanks. I'll pass," she said with much difficulty. She leaned her head against the desk and closed her eyes. She could feel his nearness from the way her skin tingled, and her heart raced from his close presence.

"Sarah?"

"Hmm?"

"Who was that man earlier today? The one you ran away from?"

Sarah let out a big sigh. He had asked. Finally. Would telling him push him away? There was only one way to find out.

CHAPTER TWENTY-FOUR

Philip was angry at himself for wanting to kiss Sarah again. He'd decided to maintain some distance between them till he got to know her more. But yet, here he was, already wanting her in his arms. Even though his ego had been bruised when she'd turned him down, she had been right to do so, and he admired her for it.

So he asked the first question that came to mind.

Sarah had her back to him the whole time she told him about the guy named Tucker. She had to clear her throat a couple of times, and her voice trembled as she spoke.

His hands curled into fists. Phillip had never wanted to kill anyone before, but in that instant, he wanted to wring the guy's neck, as well as throttle her ex-boyfriend Sean who had brought such evil into her life. By the time she was done, Sarah slumped against the desk and stayed quiet without turning, as if afraid to see his face.

Phillip put his hand out and touched her back gently. He had to be careful; she was vulnerable and skittish and would dart away if he made the wrong move.

She let out a sigh that curled its way around his heart. That's when he knew he was a goner. It didn't matter what he told himself. Sarah Nash had warmed her way back into his heart and was going nowhere. And it was in his best interests to stop fighting it.

He continued to rub her back until she turned and looked at him. Her blue-gray eyes were large, open, and clear for him to read. And Phillip saw a beautiful young lady who had been wounded time and time again, and yet was willing to give him a chance. He had hurt her earlier in the day, but she hadn't held it against him.

They stared at each other, and Phillip reached out

a hand and brushed his fingers against her cheek. Her eyes fluttered close. Phillip's breath hitched. She was perfect and beautiful, her past included. It had made her who she was. Anyone who thought otherwise was stupid.

He pulled her to him and lowered his mouth on hers. He kissed her gently at first. Her mouth tasted sweet like honeysuckle, full of goodness and tenderness, and suddenly, he couldn't get enough. But he held himself back. At that moment, it was not about him but all about her. He kissed her again, lightly on the lips, and then just held her in his arms. And they stayed that way.

Because it was what she needed.

CHAPTER TWENTY-FIVE

Sarah's hand felt warm and safe tucked into Phillip's as they entered the church for the carol service. The place was already half-full, and heads turned and voices whispered as Phillip led her to his family's pew right at the front.

Sarah tried to pull her hand away. What was Phillip thinking? If she sat there, people would assume they were engaged, which they weren't. But Phillip held her hand tightly till they entered the pew and sat down.

Geoffrey was already seated at the end of the

pew and gave Sarah a warm smile. Sarah smiled back. It was nice to see a friendly face in the room. Veronica had already told her in the morning she would be late. Even though it was Christmas Eve, her office was closing late since they wouldn't be open again until after the New Year.

Sarah looked to the pew on the other side. The children from the orphanage sat there, chattering excitedly. They would be presenting the nativity scene in tonight's Christmas carol service and were already garbed in colorful attires depicting the times of Jesus. They waved at Sarah, and she waved back. She surmised the pews would be full before the service was done. Most folks in the community were expected to attend.

The pastor came on stage and led the church in an opening prayer. And then the floor was opened to the children.

Sarah couldn't remember when she had laughed so much. The children's acting and their antics were fun to watch. Hannah, especially, was a hoot. She forgot her lines and created new ones that no one else knew about, which threw off her co-actors who scrambled to get the play back on track. The church choir led the congregation in some of their favorite

Christmas songs, and bittersweet memories washed over Sarah as she sang along. And through it all, Phillip stayed close either holding her hand or with his arm around her shoulders. Her heart was truly full, and she couldn't ask for more.

The service finally ended, and quite a number of the community rushed forward to chat with Phillip. They got separated, and for a moment, Sarah felt alone until she noticed Geoffrey standing by her side. She was grateful for his presence.

"Hey, Sarah, I've been looking for you." Sarah turned to see Veronica carrying a large tote bag.

"What in the world are you carrying?" Sarah asked.

"I bought groceries. The store won't be open tomorrow."

When Sarah turned to introduce Geoffrey, he was gone. She looked around only to see him talking to a petite lady with beautiful long hair. From his animated expressions, she figured the young woman was special to him.

"What are you looking at?" Veronica asked.

"Oh, nothing."

Veronica looked around. 'Where's Mr. Hunk?"

Sarah elbowed her. "Don't call him that. Someone

might hear you."

"But everyone knows he is a hunk. I saw how cozy you two were during the service. I take it things have progressed?"

Sarah looked away. "I don't know what you're talking about."

"Sarah, even a blind man could see you how bonded you two were."

Sarah covered her face with her hands. "This is so embarrassing."

"Get used to it. I mean, everyone in the church saw you two. See, he can't seem to take his eyes away from you, even though he's talking to someone else. And here he comes."

Sarah couldn't stop staring at Phillip's face. She could never get enough. In a few quick strides, he was by her side and linked his hands with hers. "Hello, Veronica," he said.

"Hello, Phillip. I see you've claimed my friend."

Sarah's ears grew warm. "Veronica!" she exclaimed in a lowered voice.

Veronica looked from Sarah to Phillip. "I'm happy for you two. But if you hurt her, I'll castrate you and feed you to the dogs."

"Veronica!" A few heads turned to see what was

going on. Sarah was sure her face was beet red by now.

Phillip nodded solemnly, and then the corners of his lips lifted into a smile. "I think it might be best if we leave," he said. "We seem to be drawing a lot of attention. How about I give you ladies a ride home?"

Veronica's face split into a broad smile. "Now, that would be perfect, Phillip."

●• —— •●

"I'll see you inside," Veronica said as she hopped up the stairs and into the apartment. Phillip had parked his car and now leaned against its hood beside Sarah.

"I like her," Phillip said. "She's very protective of you, and that's great to see."

Sarah couldn't agree more. "She's wonderful. One of the best friends anyone could ever have."

"I had fun today." Phillip's hand played with hers. "I'm glad you went along with my surprise."

"It was one of my best days ever. Thanks for doing it for me."

"You're welcome. You know what? I don't feel like going back to an empty home. I wish I could just stay here with you."

"But Geoffrey is there."

"Oh, he is definitely not there. Didn't you see him with someone at the church?'

"The pretty lady with the long hair? Is that his wife?"

"He's not married. Let me correct that—he will soon be."

"Does that mean he'll leave?"

"No, I doubt that. Geoffrey is part of the family, and he has his own apartment on the grounds. But at the end of the day, it will be his decision on whether to stay or go." Phillip intertwined his hand with hers. "So what are your plans for tomorrow?"

Sarah couldn't help but yawn, and she covered her mouth in embarrassment.

Phillip chuckled. "I'm guessing the plan is to sleep in?"

Sarah flashed him an apologetic smile. "I think I need that. I know it's Christmas Day and all, but a nice long sleep in the morning would be great. I'll probably head over to the orphanage in the evening for Christmas dinner. What about you?"

"I'll catch up on some work I need to take care of in preparation for the launch, and then I'll be at orphanage too."

"How's the launch prep coming along?"

"Everything is on track. I just need to work on my speech. I don't have that ready yet."

Sarah flashed him a tired smile. "I suck at speeches, so unfortunately, I can't be of much help." She yawned again.

"Okay, that's the sign that it's time for me to go." He paused to give her a grin that melted her insides. He pulled her closer in his arms until his face hovered over hers.

Sarah closed her eyes in anticipation. Phillip leaned closer and rested his forehead on hers, and then lifted his head to press a light feathery kiss on her forehead and another on her lips. "Good night, Sarah." He gave her another hug.

Sarah hugged him right back. She wished she could just stay in his arms, but it was getting very late.

He finally let her go and then rounded his car and stepped into it.

Sarah gave him a quick wave, and he motioned for her to go in. She walked up the stairs, opened the apartment door, turned back, and waved at him again.

Phillip honked twice and then drove away.

CHAPTER TWENTY-SIX

Sarah stretched on the couch as she thought about yesterday. Christmas morning had been a quiet affair. She'd slept all through the morning and woken up refreshed. She and Veronica had exchanged gifts— Sarah had given her a gift card to the department store and a set of silver spoons she'd been dying for. Veronica had gotten her a certificate for one year of weekly spa treatment, saying Sarah needed some pampering after all the hard work she'd done over the years. They had watched a cheesy Christmas movie together and then headed to the orphanage for

Christmas dinner. Sarah had resisted calling Phillip all day, knowing they would meet later, and she'd wanted no interruption of her much needed girl time with Veronica.

The dinner had been boisterous and loud, just the way she'd imagined it would be. Phillip had sat beside her and had been the perfect gentleman. The dinner itself had been delicious: there had been apricot-glazed smoke ham, roast Cornish hen, horseradish crusted beef, vegetable lasagna, sweet potatoes loaded with marshmallows, pecan and cinnamon, Italian roasted mushrooms and veggies, cranberry-almond-spinach salad, and apple-walnut stuffing.

Sarah had eaten a bit of everything and managed to still squeeze in some dessert, which included snowball cupcakes and pecan mini cheesecakes topped with ice-cream. She had blatantly refused to get up once she was done. Phillip had laughed at her and volunteered to carry her to the car.

Sarah's lips curled into a smile as she remembered the way her breath had caught in her chest when she'd seen him walk in, his soft gaze on her like no other woman existed. Her shoulder had tingled where his hand had rested throughout dinner, and the gentle pressure of his hand on her back had sent ripples through her as he'd escorted her to his car when it was time to leave. They had chatted and laughed outside Veronica's apartment till it got late, and he had to go home.

She liked Phillip a lot. The young boy she'd crushed on had grown into a wonderful young man. There was a solidness about his character, despite how wealthy he was. She liked that he was still down-to-earth and didn't think himself above others. And of course, his being so handsome didn't hurt either. And he had accepted her past and treated her like his equal, which had surprised her, considering all the other eligible young women he could have gone out with.

She looked at the time. It was already eleven-thirty a.m. She had still enough time for some pampering with a leisurely bath. She had made plans with Phillip to meet at one p.m. Just thinking about seeing him again already had butterflies dancing in her stomach.

The doorbell rang. Sarah looked up. Who could it be? Veronica had gone out with a few friends from work, so Sarah wasn't expecting anyone now. She rose and ambled to the door and looked through the peephole. A somewhat short man in a black suit sporting slicked-back hair stood outside her door.

Sarah opened the door and kept the chain-lock in place. She could see a black town car idling on the curb behind him.

"Who is it?" Sarah asked.

"I'm looking for Ms. Sarah Nash," the man said.

"Who are you?"

"Mr. Harrison would like to speak with you."

"I don't know anyone by that name." Sarah pulled the door to close it.

"Hold on. It's about Phillip Dexington."

CHAPTER TWENTY-SEVEN

Phillip looked at his speech. It wasn't quite where he would have liked it to be, but it would do for now. The launch was only three days away, and all other necessary arrangements were in place. All that remained was to give Bori a go-ahead call regarding the surgeon. Phillip would do that later tonight, since Bori had promised he would be back online by then.

He'd also taken care of some paperwork for the hospital, so he could have the afternoon free. Phillip leaned back on the swivel chair in his home office and stretched his hands behind his head.

He missed Sarah. How had she gotten all wrapped up in him? A few days ago, she hadn't been in his life, and now he couldn't wait to hear her voice. His hands were itching to call or text her. But they had already planned to meet at one p.m. And given the amount of food she had consumed, he wasn't sure if she had woken up from her food coma.

Phillip grinned as he remembered how she'd surprised everyone during the after-dinner games. She'd been a ferocious card player. He was glad he didn't gamble—he would have lost one thousand times to her. They had talked late into the night and the more he had learned about her, the more he had fallen for her.

Because, yes, he had fallen for Sarah Nash one hundred percent. She had breezed into Dexington and stolen his heart. The heart he had kept tightly wrapped up since Nicole.

He hadn't told Sarah about Nicole. He would remedy that today. He looked at his time. Maybe he would go thirty minutes early and surprise her. It would give him enough time to share about Nicole and still enjoy the afternoon with her.

Phillip picked up his wallet and called for Geoffrey.

CHAPTER TWENTY-EIGHT

Sarah sat in the booth opposite the man called Mr. Harrison—an unassuming man in a light green polo shirt and tan slacks till he'd opened his mouth, and then she'd felt like she was sitting next to a boom box.

Sarah tapped her feet while she waited to hear what he had to say. They had gone over to the coffee shop opposite Veronica's apartment, and he'd ordered a cup of coffee. Sarah had opted for water instead.

"What is it about Phillip?" she asked when the

silence dragged on for too long.

"As expected, you're on a first-name basis," Harrison said.

"What has that got to do with anything?"

Harrison leaned forward. "Let me get straight to the point. Mr. Dexington has an item I'm interested in which he plans to launch. He is in way over his head, and I would like to help him out. I need you to get that item for me."

Sarah couldn't believe what she was hearing. "Wait a second. Are you asking me to steal from Phillip?"

"Ms. Nash, right now, you have an unusual access to Phillip, which should change soon anyway. You can ask anyone in this town how many ladies have had their hearts broken by Mr. Dexington. Once he's had his fun with you, because he will, he'll have no choice but to kick you to the curb. Do you think his family would accept you?" Harrison gave a hideous laugh. "You can't tell me you expect him to marry you."

Sarah's blood boiled, and she sprang to her feet. "I don't know why I should sit here and listen to this nonsense." She picked up her purse to leave.

Mr. Harrison sipped his coffee. "Because of your

mother."

An icy fear snaked through Sarah. Her mother? Sarah's heart rate accelerated, and she sat back down. "What has my mother got to do with this?"

"I checked your background and found something interesting. Your mother should be facing criminal charges now, yet you covered for her. How long do you think it would take before she screws you over again? I guarantee it would be less than six months. And if she does, we'll report it and make sure she gets some jail time.

"You won't be the first girl to do this, you know. His ex-girlfriend, Nicole, did the same thing and made over ten million dollars and is living in comfort as we speak. You could have much more than that. Here's a first advance for the job." He slid an envelope across the table to her.

Sarah took a deep breath. So, this was the conniving scoundrel that had made sure Phillip's first invention was a failure. And Nicole was the person close to him that broke his heart. She couldn't believe Harrison had the guts to approach her after what he'd done before!

Besides, the guy didn't know that Sarah had spoken with her mom over Christmas. Her mom had realized the extent of the harm she'd caused Sarah and had apologized. She was also getting counseling and therapy.

Righteous anger swelled up and burned in Sarah. She stood to her full five-foot-seven height and glared down at Mr. Harrison. "I'm going to make say this clear only once, so please listen carefully. I'm not going to steal from Phillip, not now, and not in the future. In fact, I'm going to tell him everything you've just told me. And you can do whatever you want regarding my mother. Do not approach me ever again!" Heads swiveled from other customers in the coffee shop to look in her direction, but Sarah didn't care.

"And one word of advice," she continued. "Try and invent your own, instead of stealing from others. It's unbecoming."

With that, Sarah stormed out of the coffee shop.

CHAPTER TWENTY-NINE

Phillip parked his car outside Veronica's apartment. He'd called Sarah's phone, but it had gone to voicemail. He got out, walked to the front door, and pressed the doorbell. The bell rang from within the apartment, but there was no response. Maybe she'd gone out briefly. He sent Sarah a quick text to let her know he was at her door.

Phillip walked down the stairs and headed to his car to wait. His eyes fell on the store across the street, and he saw Sarah's familiar Californian blonde hair in a ponytail. His lips turned up in a smile. He locked his car to cross the street, and that's when he saw the last person he expected to be there.

His heart dropped to his stomach. Harrison. His arch-enemy and nemesis. The one person who was determined to steal his inventions. What was Sarah doing talking with him?

His eyes widened as he saw Harrison slip an envelope across the table to Sarah. Phillip spun around, even as his heart felt like it had been ripped apart. He had seen enough. He couldn't bear to see her final act of betrayal. How could Sarah do this to him after everything they'd shared?

Philip clutched his chest as his heart squeezed in pain. It was the Nicole situation all over again. He had been a fool to trust Sarah, to open himself up to her. He had thought she was honest, but had instead fallen hook, line, and sinker for her deception.

He had to leave. He strode to his car and opened the driver's door.

"Phillip?"

His head swiveled to look at her. His heart skipped a beat, and Phillip hated himself at that moment. For thinking she still looked adorable in her pink T-shirt and lounge pants even though she had betrayed him.

"You came early," she said, a smile on her face.

How could she pretend as if nothing had happened? His anger boiled. "I'm glad I did. If not, I would have still remained a fool."

A bewildered look flashed across Sarah's face. "Phillip, what are you talking about?"

"Don't pretend you don't know! I saw you talking to Harrison."

"It's not what you think."

"What is it then? You cavort with the enemy, and then come and play all innocent with me? And all this time you were laughing behind my back? You must have thought I was so idiotic."

Her eyes glistened with unshed tears, but Phillip refused to be moved by them. She had played him like a fiddle with those tears.

"How could you think that of me?" Sarah said. "All I've ever been was open and transparent with you. I thought these last few days were the best days of my life. But what's the point if you can't even trust me?"

Phillip strode a few steps toward her. "Sarah, don't turn this one on me."

"Don't *call* my name! I was the bigger fool to let you into my heart. Just leave, please."

"Sarah—"

"Goodbye, Phillip." She hurried into her apartment and slammed the door shut.

CHAPTER THIRTY

Phillip stood and gazed out the floor-to-ceiling windows of his home office. A pair of robins flew past, but Phillip took no notice. His mind was still on what had happened yesterday.

Sarah. He'd thought he had finally found love at last. A person who truly understood and cared for him. The kind of woman he could spend the rest of his life with. Someone who didn't care about how much money he had, and who just loved him for who he was. Who made him laugh and smile at the same time. Yes, he'd been considering declaring his love for her and proposing to her. He didn't care about Sarah's past. It was who she was now that mattered to him.

But Sarah had stabbed him in the back and twisted the knife. He'd thought he'd been hurt by Nicole, but it was nothing compared to this. His heart ached like it was about to die.

He rubbed his eyes, but the gritty feel to them remained. He'd tossed and turned last night and had gotten no sleep. If he was a drinker, this would have been the perfect time to down some bottles, but at the end he would have been worse off than he was now. And he still had his upcoming launch to take care of and the hospital business to manage. The town folks were depending on him for their livelihood. He couldn't let Sarah and Harrison take everything away from him.

His cellphone rang. Phillip strode to his desk and picked it up. It was Bori. He pressed the green button.

"Hi, Bori."

"Phillip, are you okay? Your voice sounds strange."

"I'm good. I didn't get enough sleep."

"Wow, you must have had a great day yesterday

with the little lady."

"What are you talking about?"

Phillip heard a sigh of exasperation from the other end of the line. "Phillip, I may not be in Dexington, but I have ears. I heard you've met the love of your life."

"She's not the love of my life!"

"Phillip, what's wrong? You sound different, angry."

Phillip told him all that had transpired yesterday outside Veronica's apartment. Bori was silent for a moment. "Phillip, are you sure that's what really happened?"

"Hey, I thought you were on my side!"

"Calm down, cowboy. I'm on your side, don't get me wrong. But did you talk with her?"

"I just told you what happened."

"I mean, did you hear her side of the story?"

"Well, I didn't really … I was too angry."

"Phillip, you need to go talk to her."

"I'm doing nothing of the sort." He let out a big sigh and collapsed into his swivel chair. "I mean, what if she tells me more lies? Just seeing her may make me forget what she'd done."

Bori chuckled. "That bad? Do you remember

how I misunderstood what happened with Annie? If I hadn't gone back and made things right, I would have missed out on a chance of a lifetime and the most wonderful woman I've ever known. You need to give Sarah a chance to explain."

"I don't know, Bori. Meanwhile, why did you call?"

"What's your decision regarding Dr. Greene? I waited for your call last night."

"Sorry about that. I had a lot on my mind."

"You really did. So what's the verdict? Yay or nay?"

"Let's go ahead with him."

"Awesome. I'll let Dr. Greene know right away. He might even want to fly in tomorrow and see you."

"That's fine. Did you hear back from the FDA folks?"

"We are all set with the FDA. You should check your email, an electronic version of the license was sent to you. The paper copy will arrive in the mail. And I haven't heard anything else about Harrison."

"That's great."

"So think about what I said. Go talk to Sarah."

"Goodbye, Bori. My regards to Annie."

"Alright. I'll talk to you later." The line went dead.

Phillip got up and strolled to the window. Yes, he was miserable without Sarah. Bori might have made some sense, but he wasn't sure whether he was ready to risk his heart again. It might not survive any further damage.

And besides, he needed everything he had in him right now to focus on the upcoming launch.

CHAPTER THIRTY-ONE

Phillip walked around the ballroom shaking hands with the doctors that had come forward to congratulate him. The launch for Arthrodev had been a success. His team had really come together to make it happen.

And he'd been worried for nothing. Dr. Greene had been a seasoned professional. He'd flown in a day before and had discussed Arthrodev extensively with Phillip, Dexington Healthcare's product development team, and its team of physician advisors. Dr. Greene was confident that the product would meet a current gap in the devices for full knee transplant. Phillip planned to reach out to him in the future once they had more products in the pipeline. He was glad he had listened to Bori.

He walked out to the balcony and took a deep breath. There was no one else here, and he was glad for the solitude. Even though tonight had been wonderful, something had been absent and he knew why.

He missed Sarah Nash with a deep ache that refused to go away. He didn't know whether he would ever be free of her. He had dreamed of sharing this night with her, its success being theirs together. And maybe Bori was right about listening to what she had to say. Phillip would still be devastated if she lied to him again, but that was still better than living like a dead man because she was no longer in his life.

"Well, well, well, Phillip. You seem to have outdone yourself this time around." Phillip turned to see Harrison with a drink in his hand.

A muscle in Phillip's jaw twitched. "Hello, Harrison. What are you doing here? I don't recall sending you an invite for this party."

"I have my ways. And besides, you invited all the physician groups in the area, and I do own some of them."

"Well, enjoy yourself." Phillip turned to walk away.

"This must be your lucky year, Phillip. A good product and a good woman. Sarah Nash is one of a kind." Harrison gave a mirthless chuckle. "She didn't even blink when I tried to blackmail her. First woman who has ever stood up to me. I don't see her around. Where is she?"

Phillip froze. "What do you mean you black-mailed her?"

"She didn't tell you? I offered her some good money and threatened to have her mother arrested if she refused. But she didn't back down."

Phillip moved closer to Harrison. "You threat-ened her mother?" Anger surged in him and he threw a punch in Harrison's face.

"What the—?" Are you crazy? I'll sue you for this. Bori, you saw that."

Phillip turned to see Bori shrug and step across the threshold into the balcony.

"I didn't see anything," Bori said. "Phillip, you might want to head out. I'll handle the rest of the party. And Harrison."

"Thanks." Phillip squeezed Bori's shoulder and hastened out, leaving Harrison sputtering in the background.

He had to find Sarah Nash.

He just hoped he wasn't too late.

●● ● —— ● ●

Phillip hurried up the steps of Veronica's apartment and pressed the doorbell. Its shrill note pierced the air loud and clear from inside the apartment, but no one came to the door. He pressed down on it again but longer this time. He heard the jangling sound of door chain being unhooked before the door opened and Veronica stood in front of him, her hands on her hips. A frown creased her face.

"Are you trying to disturb the whole neighborhood?" she asked.

"Hello, Veronica. I'm looking for Sarah."

Veronica crossed her arms. "And why would that be?"

"I just want to talk to her."

Veronica smiled sweetly through clenched teeth. "I told you I would castrate you if you ever hurt Sarah. Would you like to wait around and find out if that's going to happen?"

"Veronica, I didn't know—"

'You didn't ask, did you? You passed judgement

all by your uppity self. If you think you can just waltz in here and talk to her, you have another thing coming."

"I'm sorry, I hurt her."

"Hurt her? That's an understatement. You broke her heart. You tore it out, and fed it to the dogs. I had never seen her cry so hard—I was literally scared for her. She was so dejected, like she'd given up."

Phillip's heart ached at what he had done. This was worse than he'd imagined.

"I thought better of you, Phillip," Veronica continued. "I'm so disappointed in you."

"Listen, Veronica. I'll do anything, anything to make it up to her." Phillip ran his hands through his hair. "I'm going crazy here. I've called her number over and over, but she's not picking up. Even if it takes the rest of my life, I'm willing to make it up to her."

"Really?"

"I'm serious. I'm prepared to ask her to marry me. Please, Veronica."

Veronica's eyes searched Phillip's face. Then she sighed. "I'm going to go against my better judgement here, just because I had high hopes for both of you. But I will kill you if you mess this up."

"Thanks, Veronica."

She let out a long exhale. "She's on her way to catch a flight back to California. If you hurry, maybe you might be able to stop her."

"Thank you, thank you!" Phillip hurried down the steps.

"Don't thank me yet!" Veronica called after him. "Just make sure you bring her back!"

CHAPTER THIRTY-TWO

Sarah dragged her carry-on behind her as she headed toward the airport terminal doors. It was late in the day; most flights had arrived and departed, and the area was somewhat empty. She'd been able to snag a last-minute ticket to Los Angeles at the curbside counter. Veronica had begged her to wait till the next day. But everything around Sarah had reminded her of Phillip, and she couldn't take it anymore. She had checked her other bags at the counter. Veronica had agreed to send Betty to her once she arrived back in LA. All that was left was to go through security.

"Sarah!" a familiar voice called out.

It couldn't be him. He was supposed to be at his launch party, which was also why she had planned to leave at this time. She wouldn't be tempted to run to him.

"Sarah!" She turned to see Phillip racing toward her, wearing a black tuxedo that molded onto his body.

Her heart raced. It was really him. She turned back toward the terminal entrance and hurried her steps.

A hand grabbed her arm. Sarah felt the familiar tingle course through her body. "Sarah, please," Phillip said.

Sarah knocked his hand off. "What do you want, Phillip? Haven't you done enough?"

"I'm sorry, Sarah."

Sarah's eyes blazed. "You are sorry? I don't ever want to see you again."

"Please, Sarah. Let me make it up to you."

"So now you know you were wrong." Sarah jabbed a finger at his chest. "I opened my heart to you, I showed you everything about me. But what did you do? You accused me. You didn't even bother to hear me out. Didn't you at least doubt for a second what you saw? You should have given me the benefit of the doubt. I deserved that much."

Phillip ran his hands through his hair. "I shouldn't have judged you through what I had experienced before."

"Right. The experience that you never told me about. I'd shared everything about me, but yet you couldn't tell me about something so important. You didn't trust me, Phillip."

"Sarah, I came early that day just to tell you about it. I really did. I'm sorry. Please give me another chance. I promise I'll make it up to you."

"For the record, I defended you to that lout called Harrison. I stood up for you, so imagine how I felt when you turned your back on me."

"It's all my fault. Please forgive me."

Sarah's chest heaved as she stared at Phillip. He took a gingerly step toward her and then another.

Sarah couldn't move, and her breath caught in her chest. His familiar spicy woody scent enveloped her first, and then his arms wrapped around her. "I'm sorry, Sarah. I love you so much," he whispered against her ear.

And that did it. Waves of sobs wracked her body, and she couldn't hold back the tears from falling.

His arms tightened around her. "I promise to spend my life making it up to you," he said.

"You hurt me, Phillip, you really did. I didn't know what to do with myself," she muttered in a shaky voice in between sobs.

His hand rubbed her back. "I'll never leave you again." He leaned back and stared into her eyes as his fingers brushed her cheeks. His lips were a mere whisper away, and his eyes mesmerized hers. "I love you, Sarah Nash, will you marry me?"

Sarah's eyes widened in shock, and her breath caught in her chest.

"Breathe, Sarah, breathe," Phillip said, his eyes full of concern.

Sarah took a deep inhale and then exhaled. She found her voice. "What did you say?"

"Will you marry me and make me the happiest man ever? I promise to love you, trust you, honor you, love your mother—"

"Yes!" And she stood on tiptoes and kissed him. He crushed her against himself and kissed her right back.

Everything else faded away. It was just the two of them, with his arms wrapped around her so tightly like he'd never let go. His scent flooded her senses and she couldn't think straight.

"Sarah," he whispered, savoring her name as his lips pressed against hers in desperation. His hand reached for her ponytail and pulled off the hair tie, letting her hair fall in waves around her face.

A fire started in her belly and spread through her body as he deepened the kiss. The butterflies in her stomach went into a frenzy. She loved this man and all she wanted was to stay in his arms forever.

"Phillip! What are you doing?"

"Mother?"

CHAPTER THIRTY-THREE

Sarah froze. Mother? Sarah opened her eyes to see a middle-aged beautiful lady— with every strand of her platinum blonde hair sculptured in place— in a cream cocktail dress covered by an exaggerated-style black overcoat and her neck graced with a gray fur stole. She stood beside a tall, distinguished-looking man in a long grey coat. They looked like royalty. Sarah could see where Phillip had inherited his looks.

She dropped her arms from around Phillip. His mother had just caught her kissing her son in public! But she noticed Philip still kept his arm nested at the small of her back.

"Hello Mother, Father," he said. "What are you doing here?"

This was even worse. Correction—in front of both his parents. Sarah wished the ground would just open up and swallow her.

"Won't you give your dear mother a kiss before the twenty questions?"

Phillip let go of Sarah and stepped forward to kiss his mother on the cheek.

"Phillip, who do we have here?" his mother asked.

Phillip stepped back to grab Sarah's hand and pulled her to his side.

"Mother, Father. This is Sarah Nash, the woman I want to marry. Sarah meet my parents, Alex and Helen Dexington."

"Nice to meet you both," Sarah said. She didn't know whether to curtsy or bow.

"Marry?" his parents said in unison.

Sarah pinched Phillip's hand. Wrongest thing to say on the first meeting. "Ouch," Phillip said, rubbing his other hand over the tender spot.

"Are you okay?" his mother asked with concern.

"I'm fine. Just a little bug."

Sarah hid a smile. Bug indeed.

"Maybe we should find somewhere indoors to sit down," his father said looking around.

"Why don't we go home, Mother?"

"Why, yes, that would work best," she responded.

Phillip leaned toward Sarah. "Let's go. I'll send someone to get your checked bags."

Sarah's palms grew sweaty and she flashed them a weak smile. What if Phillip's parents didn't like her?

This might turn out to be a horrible meet-the-parents date.

● ● ● ——— ● ●

Sarah sat on the couch and twiddled her fingers. They had arrived back at Dexington House, and Philip's parents sat in the couch opposite her. Phillip had gone up to change out of his tux and now came back down wearing a grey cashmere sweater with cream slacks.

Sarah smoothened her unruly hair and tried to put it in some form of order as Phillip sat down beside her.

"Leave it alone. You look great," Phillip whispered into her ear.

"So, Phillip, maybe you should introduce her," his

father said.

Sarah jumped up. "I'm sorry, Mr. and Mrs. Dexington, but this is super awkward, and it might be better if I came back another time."

"It's Alex and Helen," his father answered and then turned to his mother. "Right, dear?"

"Yes," Helen said. "Please sit down. I'm sure it can't be as awkward as kissing my son in public. They were both ready to eat each other, isn't that so, Alex?"

"Mom!" Phillip said.

Sarah covered her face with her hands. Playing dead would have been much easier.

"See, Alex, first time he's calling me mom," Helen said.

"I know, never heard it before," Alex responded

Sarah kept her face buried and refused to look up. Right now, she needed a rescue team.

"Mother, will you please stop?" Phillip said. "And why are you back so early?"

"We heard from Geoffrey that you needed help. That you were about to make the biggest mistake of your life. Isn't that so, dear?"

Alex nodded."Yes, that's what he said. That you were about to let the most wonderful woman in your life slip away, and we needed to come back and knock some sense into you."

Sarah couldn't believe her ears. She lifted her head and looked at Phillip's parents. They were smiling. She glanced at Phillip. He had a dazed look on his face.

"So, Sarah Nash, welcome to the family." Helen got up and gave Sarah a hug. "I'm glad my son came to his senses. And I remember you from many years ago."

"You do?" Sarah and Phillip said in unison.

"Of course, you were the girl my son kissed near the pond in the orphanage. I can see you guys are still on it. The public kissing, I mean."

"Mother!"

Helen grinned. "So tell me, how did you propose? One knee, flowers…" At Phillip's blank stare, "Don't tell me you did *nothing*?"

"Mother—"

"Phillip Dexington, I taught you better." She slipped a stunning diamond petaled ring from her finger. "Now take this ring and propose to her properly. It's a family heirloom passed from fathers to their first sons. Your father proposed to me with it."

Phillip took the ring from his mother and went

down on one knee. "Sarah Nash, the most beautiful woman in the whole world, would you do me the honor and marry me?"

Sarah's throat went dry. She couldn't believe she was here, being proposed to by a man she adored, and sitting with a family that liked her.

"Yes," she said quietly and held out her hand.

Phillip slipped the ring on her finger and kissed it. It was a perfect fit. He got up and pulled her to him and gave her a kiss that made Sarah's toes curl and blossomed hope, love, joy, and happiness in her.

"Oh stuff it! Alex, I think we better leave them alone. These kids are at it again."

Sarah smiled and continued kissing the man she loved.

The one who had caught her heart and made her whole again.

EPILOGUE

Sarah sat on the porch chair and let out a sigh of contentment. Life couldn't be better. The air was peaceful, the birds were chirping, she had a cup of cocoa in her hand, and the man she loved by her side.

"Are you okay?" Phillip asked from beside her.

Sarah turned to look at him. She still couldn't believe it. That the most gorgeous man in the world was going to be her husband. Phillip's parents had announced their engagement in the papers the very next day and congratulations had flooded in. Veronica had been over the moon and promptly claimed her spot as the maid-of-honor. Sarah had called her mom that night to let her know, and she'd been happy for her. She'd promised to come down for the wedding.

Phillip had declared that he wanted to marry her as soon as possible. Sarah had insisted that she'd always wanted a holiday wedding. And since they both agreed it would be torture to wait a whole year, they had decided to marry on New Year's Day. The town would celebrate for a week while they went for their honeymoon, destination yet unknown. Phillip had insisted it would be a surprise.

The whole town was bubbling with excitement, and Dexington House buzzed with activity like never before. Helen was definitely in her element, orchestrating everything.

Sarah and Phillip had snuck out for some peace and quiet and had ended up on the back porch at the orphanage.

She flashed him a smile. "I'm good," she said as she intertwined her hand with his. Her heart was full.

"I have a wedding present for you." Phillip pulled out an envelope and handed it to her.

"What is it?" Sarah let go of his hand and tore open the envelope. A single letter fell out. She opened it and read it. Her eyes widened in surprise.

"Phillip, you didn't."

"Yes, I opened a college trust fund for the orphanage. And it's just the beginning. After what you went through, I knew you wouldn't want another kid to struggle to pay for college. And what better place than to start with these precious kids? Since it's important that the right person manage the investment portfolio, I figured you'd be the best person for it. Congratulations, Sarah Dexington, Director of Investments at The Dexington Foundation."

She stuttered. "But I still need to earn my CFA and gain more experience."

"I'm sure you'll ace it, love. And Elizabeth has agreed to serve as your mentor and advisor."

Sarah didn't know what else to say. Suddenly, snow flakes began to drop from the sky and soon covered the backyard. It was perfect.

Christmas had brought her the best man she had ever known.

The best gift ever.

Her very own Billionaire Inventor.

Thank you so much for reading!

Want to know what happens next in Dexington? Sign up now at dobidaniels.com.

If you've loved reading HER BILLIONAIRE IN-VENTOR, Dobi would be grateful if you could spend a few minutes to leave a review (as short as you like) on the book's Amazon page. Your review would help bring it to the attention of other readers. Thank you very much.

Check out all Dobi Daniels books at smarturl.it/DobiDaniels.

ACKNOWLEDGMENTS

Writing a book is harder and more rewarding than I could have ever imagined. And it would not have been possible without the support, love, and encouragement from my number one cheerleader, my dearest mom. My life would never have been this awesome and wonderful without you.

Of course, I have to thank my precious little DC for his smiles and antics. You brighten my day and give me the strength to keep pushing through.

Thank you to my sisters for encouraging me on this wonderful journey. And a special thanks to my baby brother (who is so not a baby anymore) for being super supportive and checking in on my progress. You guys are the best.

Thank you to my wonderful author friends. You know who you are. Your selflessness and willingness to share what you know has made my writing journey smoother and an exciting one.

Most of all, I want to thank God who gave me life, surrounded me with the most wonderful people, and loved me all the way. You make my life complete.

And finally, a special thanks to all my readers whose love of my stories spur me on to write more. Thank you!

ABOUT DOBI DANIELS

As a former physician and business executive in another life—with a childhood filled with reading multi-genre novels—Dobi Daniels loves to write thrilling stories with heart. Whether it'd be romance, or whatever book that takes her fancy, Dobi Daniels loves to dream up and pen everyday characters that rise above unfavorable circumstances to overcome incredible odds and find joy along the way.

Her Billionaire Inventor is the first book in the Dexington Medical Billionaire Romance Series. Sign up at dobidaniels.com to be notified when the next book in the series comes out!

Thank you!

www.dobidaniels.com
hello@dobidaniels.com
smarturl.it/DobiDaniels_BookBub
smarturl.it/DobiDaniels_FB

Made in the USA
San Bernardino, CA
24 May 2019